Then, after the accident there and at the end of that summer, he answered again the obscure call and vanished into the wilderness of the south. "I wish I knew where I was going," he wrote Jeanne Carr at the outset of that long walk. " 'Doomed to be carried of the spirit into the wilderness,' I suppose. I wish I could be more moderate in my desires, but I cannot, and so there is no rest." In the Sierra years to follow, he indeed died to the world of humankind and found his creative context amidst granite boulders, glaciers, bears, and birds.

THIS IS EXCELLENT. MY ONLY SUGGESTION MIGHT BE TO SHORTEN THE COLUMN BY TWO LINES.

R

tains the world's weary roar was only a rumor he heard occasionally from visitors—travelers' tales of strife in the dusty places far below. And he found confirmation

...will be lovely.

A River Dream

A River Dream

The Writing and Art of Russell Chatham's Clark City Press

EDITED BY JAMIE HARRISON

GODINE
Boston

Published in 2025 by
GODINE
Boston, Massachusetts
www.godine.com

ISBN 978-1-56792-799-3 (hardcover) | ISBN 978-1-56792-800-6 (ebook)

Library of Congress Print LCCN: 2025013082

First Printing, 2025
Printed in the United States

In memory of Russell Chatham.

And of Anne Garner,
who made beautiful books more beautiful,
and of John Fryer,
the spirit of the place.

Contents

POEMS & FICTION

ART & MISCELLANY

THE LAST CATALOGUE

A River Dream

Introduction

RUSSELL CHATHAM, while primarily known as a landscape painter, was also a printmaker, a restaurateur, and a world-class fly fisherman. He was a talented cook, a heavy drinker, an unabashed lover of women, and a rotten businessman. He married three times, owned many old cars, and during the five decades he spent in Livingston, Montana, employed a solid percentage of town. He wanted everything—*everything*—to be peerless, and he wanted to control each detail. If he could have milled the wood in his frames, he would have. If he could have printed his books on-site, with inks and paper of his own making, he would have. When he couldn't buy a good meal in town, he bought a restaurant.

And between 1986 and 2009, off and on and more or less, he was an enthusiastic book publisher, producing three dozen volumes of poetry and novels and collections of essays and photography and art at Clark City Press (CCP), some of them passion projects, most of them by friends, almost all of them graced by his own paintings, which he gave his authors in lieu of cash advances. Those authors, in the beginning, were a core group of friends he'd fished with for years: Thomas McGuane, William "Gatz" Hjortsberg, Guy de la Valdène, Dan Gerber, and Jim Harrison, who was my father.

Russell Chatham began painting because of his family. His grandfather was the great muralist and plein air painter Gottardo Piazzoni; Russell remembered watching Piazzoni paint, and he was there when his grandfather dropped dead with a brush in his hand (which may or may not be a fib on Russ's part, but I'd like to accept it). He began writing fishing essays—for money, for the excuse to fish—in his early twenties, and only fell into full-blown obsession, and something as insane as starting an independent press, because of the people he met in the late sixties. They changed his life, and he changed theirs.

Guy de la Valdène described Tom McGuane as acting like a fulcrum, and the Rube Goldberg causality goes something like this: In 1961, Jim Harrison and Thomas McGuane met each other at Michigan State University. In the fall of 1962, McGuane and William "Gatz" Hjortsberg met at the Yale School of Drama, and in 1967 they moved to Bolinas with their families, the McGuanes from Palo Alto, where Tom had been a Stegner Fellow, and the Hjortsbergs from Saint Croix. In Bolinas, they met Richard Brautigan, and they also met a fisherman and painter named Russell Chatham. The McGuanes traveled to Livingston in 1968 and left the fog of Bolinas for good in 1969, as did the Hjortsbergs. Russell and Richard Brautigan visited and followed, with Russell leasing a house on Deep Creek in the spring of 1972, and Richard buying a place near Gatz at Pine Creek. Tom, meanwhile, began to fish in the Keys, and Jim Harrison (who had visited Tom in Montana, and who by then was talking with Dan Gerber about starting the journal *Sumac*) brought his family for a visit to the McGuanes on Summerland Key. In 1969, Woody Sexton introduced Tom to Guy de la Valdène; in 1970, on another trip south, Jim met Guy. In the spring of 1971, Jim met Russ. And in the fall of 1972, Guy and Russell began a tradition of visiting Jim every October in northern Michigan, which is when I met both of them.

After meeting Tom and Gatz in Bolinas, Russell began to think differently about writing. In a 2003 interview with John A. Murray in *The Bloomsbury Review*, he said that "I knew novels were far beyond what I could do, but I thought I could do something. Having fished with uncommon ferocity for so long, I figured I could write about that, especially since I'd just caught the world-record striped bass on a fly. Surely there was a story there, and there was. I sold several pieces to magazines like *Salt Water Sportsman*, *Field & Stream*, and so forth, and on the sixth or seventh try, got one accepted by *Sports Illustrated*. And suddenly I was making my living as a writer."

I came to Livingston, after two visits as a teenager, in May of 1987, lured by the memory of a beautiful place and cheap housing and the desire to leave New York after five years of food and magazine work, and a short stint as a script editor. Russell had talked me into the idea during a visit to Michigan the previous fall, plying me with wine and grouse and god knows what else. He'd bought a house in town, and the Deep Creek homestead was available for $150 a month.

So we came. My husband and I spent the summer blowing our puny savings, and that August Russell started muttering about having some framing and proofreading work for me. His period of domestication and the move to town was only temporary but understandable all around—his daughter Rebecca was a few months old, and Russ and his third wife, Suzanne Porter, were trying to build up a business with lithographs. He was working at a press in Seattle called Ink on Paper, with a talented pressman named Chuck Matson, and they produced a stunning, austere series called *The Yellowstone River Suite* as well as some almost Japanese etchings with names like *Evening* and *Afternoon* before beginning work on a massive series called *The Missouri Headwaters*. The three-by-four-foot lithos were named for the months; to help sell them, Russell printed a companion catalogue with the help of Laurel Desnick, who also worked as a framer with an assistant named Stacy Sandler (then Feldmann, and still the most competent person I know). Russ had already reprinted a small book of his paintings originally released by Larry Winn, in Seattle; he now wanted to create a larger-format book of paintings (which would become *One Hundred Paintings*), and he also wanted to reprint the fishing anthologies he'd put out the previous decade with Nick Lyons—*Silent Seasons* (1974) and *The Angler's Coast* (1976)—and put out a new collection (*Dark Waters*).

And there I was, an English major with some peripheral print experience, in need of employment. Stacy, who had some peripheral design and very different production experience (her mother was the costume and set designer Franne Lee), began to split her time between the art wing at the west end of the office, above Sax & Fryer, and my early Apple computer and dot matrix printer at the east end, above the corner of Main and Callender. We found books about book production and design and typefaces. We found a designer—Anne Garner—and a top-notch typesetter and design company, Wilsted & Taylor. I read the *Chicago Manual of Style*. My attorney husband, Steve Potenberg, took a crash course in contracts; there were plenty of writers' contracts available for research in Livingston. Stacy and I learned how to bid out books and work page counts and pick cover stock. We asked people incredibly stupid questions, but not enough of them. We found, eventually, a distributor.

Within a matter of months, Russ's plans expanded beyond *Silent Seasons* and *Dark Waters* to include my father's earlier poetry collection with Winn Books, *The Theory & Practice of Rivers*, Dan Gerber's *Grass Fires*, and two children's books by a San Francisco artist named Wolo, whose stories Russ had loved in childhood.

When I say Russ's vision "expanded," it's hard to put across his enthusiasm and his capacity for acceleration. Whether talking about food, or a book, or a painting, or a woman, he would rub his hands together, and roll his eyes, and wave his arms wildly like a conductor in a silent movie, before he headed off to paint again and pay for it all, leading with the nose. More, more, more. In *The Bloomsbury Review* interview, Russ said, "Basically, it started because I wanted to get several of my own books back into print, and I didn't want to do business in New York any longer. I wasn't interested in proving anything; I just wanted my books available in a format entirely of my own choosing. There was no business plan, no distribution plan, no nothing. Gradually, books by a few other authors joined mine, and within a couple of short years it was decided to try and see if a, quote unquote, normal publishing business could survive in a small town in Montana. Some financial backing was found, and a staff of six hired."

It wasn't that simple. We had two full-time people with several helping part-time, three when Cindy Murphy came on to deal with billing and bookkeeping. We put out the first eight books and two catalogues and went to our first ABA before more people came on.

Looking over (largely unprintable) letters from the time, what comes through most strongly is the arrogance and the optimism: If you don't know anything it a) allows you to think you know everything, and b) allows you to think big. *One Hundred Paintings*, printed in Hong Kong and timed for a 1990 exhibition at the Museum of the Rockies, seemed to bob along forever on the Pacific. I edited *Making Game* while pregnant and *A Voice from the River* and *Querencia* with a colicky newborn. *Just Before Dark* and *The Ninemile Wolves* made money, or at least broke even, as did *Death and the Good Life* and *The Muddy Fork* and Barry Gifford's books. Russ hated being limited to paperbacks, but the press's financial ruination wasn't as simple as the incredibly expensive trio of *One Hundred Paintings*, *The Angler's Coast*, and *Law of the Range.*[1] By now we had Kevin Morrissey for marketing, the only professional in the mix, but no one could talk Russ out of anything until we ran out of money, and we went ahead with the printing of *Peter Stackpole: Life in Hollywood.*

Many people tried to lend guidance, though Russ came in for considerable grief from Seymour "Sam" Lawrence, Jim and Tom and Rick Bass's publisher at Houghton Mifflin, a collector of Russell's paintings and a sometime partaker of the messy trips to Key West. Sam varied between thinking of the press as a threat and a joke, and he was merciless in his letters.

Dan Gerber, forever patiently helping the press through financial crises, made the hiring of his friend Tim Gable, who'd been a manager at Borders in Detroit, a condition of a new loan in 1992 ("my potential investment in CCP is designed to give it a reasonable chance of business success, not simply to help it limp along for another year or two"). Tim, as the new managing editor, was to call the shots, but he called nothing, in the end, and doubled down on more hardcovers and art books. He brought along the wonderful Jan Kimmel as shipping manager (and proofreader, and doer of a dozen other tasks) and hired a publicist, who left after a disastrous ABA in Anaheim that included a fight at a rooftop Atlantic Monthly Press party. During the convention, after Jack Shoemaker (then at Pantheon) told me I had to get a grip on the publicist, I was so demoralized that I burst into tears when I saw Jimmy Carter—apparently the last decent human on the planet—signing books.

David Streitfeld wrote a contemporary account in a 1991 *Washington Post* article:

> Clark City began about three years ago, when Chatham, who is primarily a painter but also known for his essays and articles on the outdoors, republished a volume of his own work. [Harrison] came on board about that time, in flight with her lawyer husband from New York City. She had known Chatham since she was a kid but had no background in book publishing.

1 Diana Guest's *Stonecarver* was partly subsidized by her family; *A River Runs Through It* was a work for hire.

> "We underestimated just how much it costs to start out, how long it takes to really start generating money," she says. "This is not a big profit business at the best of times." It took a year to put out the first two books. "I can't stress too much," she says, "how little we knew."
>
> Now they're aiming at about eight a year . . . . Clark City has ambitious plans to do books of all types, from poetry and short stories to a children's book . . . . "We're doing books that are closer to the author's heart, but potentially less profitable to a major New York house," [Harrison says].

Or just less profitable! Anyway, we had fun, most of the time, until we didn't.

Life and art, life as art: One of Russ's oldest and most perceptive friends, the artist Etel Adnan (whose work he hoped to publish at Clark City), contributed an introduction to the first printed collection of his art (*Russell Chatham*, Winn Press, 1984; Clark City Press, 1987) and wrote of meeting him in the sixties: "Chatham, too, was an angry young man, one of the angriest maybe, and happily so, laughing and drinking as if life were a mythology. But his anger was expressed in his determination to follow his own destiny, to say what he had to say (and to see) in ways then not in fashion, to be concerned to an absolute degree with the integrity of the work."

She was, of course, writing about Russell the painter. The austerity of the landscapes she and Chris Waddington celebrated in their essays never extended to food or love. Russell as an artist and friend was brilliant and joyful and hugely melancholic, but if I were going to describe Russell as a businessman the first term would be *enthusiasm*. The second would be *oversubscribed*, or possibly *in debt*. If he had it, he spent it. I keep hoping that the sample budget he sent out to his friends in the mid-seventies will turn up someday—thousands of dollars on flowers, food, wine, etc. After Clark City, his dissatisfaction with local dining options forced him to open the Livingston Bar & Grille, an undertaking even more financially ruinous than the press, but wonderful fun for everyone he knew. He flew Poilâne bread in from Paris, shipped grouper and snapper in from the Gulf (trading several beautiful oils for fish from Charles and Carla Morgan's Harbor Docks), and generally failed to adequately mark up his wine or his caviar. I earned my last five-star hangover with Guy de la Valdène and a bottle of Germain Robin in one of those banquettes.

Toward the end, things were often difficult on many levels. Russell was married to three women and had four beautiful children before his last long relationship with Elizabeth Blavatsky, but his life was not an uninterrupted lovefest. During the Clark City period, his wife Suzanne, who had her own staff in the same offices above Sax & Fryer, managed Russell's art sales and had to watch him spend that money on the press and other pursuits. Memos were written and affections flamed out.

The end proper: Without wading too far into the mess, by the late fall of 1992, it became clear that for the press to continue, Russ would need to give up full control, and we worked at various scenarios. I talked to Morgan Entrekin of Grove Atlantic in December 1992, when I went to New York for a sales conference and to talk to Peter Matthiessen about *Red & Blue Days*; other interested parties included Wilsted & Taylor, the incredible typesetting and design company in Berkeley that was a joy to work with.

Russ wouldn't, in the end, accept any limits on control. It was his press, and it would stay that way. He'd warned us in a memo.

> I intend to run the company and if I find I can't do that for whatever reason, it will close down. I started this purely for the sake of fun and satisfaction. If it turns into something largely unpleasant I don't need it.

We spent the next weeks getting the typeset books already in production to new homes: Bruce Cutler's *The Massacre at Sand Creek* to the University of Oklahoma, Merrill Gilfillan's *Sworn Before Cranes* to Orion, Rebecca Newth's *Great North Woods* to Will Hall Books, Jon Jackson's *Go by Go* to Dennis McMillan, and Michael Katakis's *Sacred Trusts* (Tim Gable's project; he was also working on a novel by Laura Seager), which ended up at Mercury House. Peter Matthiessen, at work on the *Killing Mister Watson* trilogy, never went back to *Red & Blue Days*.

It all hurt, especially Peter's book—I'd written my undergraduate thesis about him. It felt like we were on the verge of finally being viable, though people always feel like they're winning at cards, don't they? In the large category of books I wished we'd been able to publish, there were several food projects—we had talked to Ari Weinzweig about a Zingerman's cookbook, and Shelley Boris, a manager of Dean & DeLuca, was working on recipes; Guy, Russ, and Jim planned to do a cookbook together, as well. I have notes on an anthology of the great female cookbook authors, and we intended to reprint Toulouse-Lautrec's beautiful *The Art of Cuisine* (which Henry Holt republished a few years later).

Terry Tempest Williams was thinking of "something about women and wild animals"; P. J. O'Rourke wanted to place some essays. Dan O'Brien had a novel, Judith Freeman had some novellas, Rick Bass had a grizzly book, and so did Doug Peacock, who also wanted to write an introduction to a new edition of Edward Abbey's *Slickrock*. James Lee Burke was thinking of rewriting his first novel, *Half of Paradise*.

Russell wanted to publish Ted Trueblood's essays and B. Kliban's *Dancers* and his own *Striped Bass on the Fly*. He wanted to celebrate Etel Adnan. He intended to put out a big book of his grandfather Gottardo Piazzoni's paintings and murals, as well as the commercial art of Maurice Del Mue, his uncle. There was talk of Tom McGuane's screenplays and Richard Brautigan's *An Unfortunate Woman*. Guy had a quail book, and Frederick Turner suggested Lucile Adler's "The Red Pear Tree" and wanted to rewrite *Of Chiles, Cacti, and Fighting Cocks*. Rick DeMarinis signed on for *A Lovely Monster* and *Cinder*; Joseph Bednarik, now copublisher of Copper Canyon Press, ultimately published *The Sumac Reader* with Michigan State University Press. I have notes about Louise Erdrich short stories, a Walter Kirn mystery, *A Writer's Guide to the Rockies/West Coast*, Kathryn Marshall's never finished "Cyanide Waltz," and an anthology project of writers' notebooks with some biggish names. We talked about reprints of William Hjortsberg's *Falling Angel*, Knut Hamsun's *Victoria*, Hugh Nissenson's *The Tree of Life*, Harry Crews's *A Childhood*, Donald McCaig's *The Butte Polka*, Charles Willeford's *I Was Looking for a Street*, Mark Smith's *The Death of the Detective*, and Ray A. Young Bear's *Black Eagle Child*.

When I started writing this introduction, I struggled with how to describe these writers, not just in terms of their talents but in terms of my relationships with them. I met Tom McGuane when I was a baby, Dan Gerber when I was seven or eight, Guy and Russ when I was about twelve. It's impossible for me to give a dry, factual introduction to any of them, and after a few attempts, I've given up trying. They were all wonderful to me as a child, and they were my friends as an adult. Obviously, I lack editorial distance.

Clark City was a small world, and it's a lost world, and from a three-decade distance, it was an objectively insane undertaking, and it devoured a chunk of my life. I'm proud of the learning curve and the quality and the beauty of the books, but not all of them are the books I'd print or buy or read now.

In the aftermath of Russ's shutting down the press, I'll admit that I was enraged, and openly found fault, and Russ wasn't inclined to enjoy or even acknowledge criticism or failure. We still ate together and talked to each other over the years, but almost always within a larger group. Kevin Morrissey eventually found work as the marketing and sales manager for the Minnesota Historical Society Press, and he was the managing editor of the *Virginia Quarterly Review* from 2004 to 2010, when he took his own life. Stacy Sandler found work at *The Livingston Enterprise* but eventually moved back to Madison, Wisconsin, where she ultimately became the president of a wine distribution company.

I floundered before I went on three months of unemployment and wrote a mystery novel, sold it, and wrote three more. Occasionally, I'd hear rumors that Russ was restarting the press, and in 2001, Clark City began a second life with editor Sally Epps (then O'Connor). They printed poetry by Charles Levendosky and Ed Lahey, as well as Lahey's novel *The Thin Air Gang* and Keith Wilson's *Shaman of the Desert*. They produced Ellen Crain and Janet L. Finn's incredible anthology *Motherlode: Legacies of Women's Lives and Labors in Butte, Montana*; *The Range of Memory* (about the Teton Range, with photos from Ed Riddell and short passages by Terry Tempest Williams); the anthology *The River We Carry with Us* (about the Clark Fork basin, edited by Emily Miller and Tracy Stone-Manning, the future director of the Bureau of Land Management); *Mile High Mile Deep* by Richard K. O'Malley (O'Malley wrote this memory of a childhood in Butte while he was Paris bureau chief for the AP in the sixties); and two memoirs (*The*

Berkeley Pit by Dorothy Bryant and *For All Time* by Helen Claypool). Other volumes in this later era: *Art Flick: Catskill Legend* by Roger Keckeissen and *A Moon Over Wings*, poetry by Thomas Aslin.

But Russell and I had come away with different lessons from the death of the first press, beyond agreeing that starting in complete ignorance was unwise. Russell, in the *Bloomsbury* interview, took away a different moral of the story than I did, saying of the second iteration of the press, in 2003:

> Aside from being appropriately modest, it will operate largely outside the parameters which govern most other presses. There will be no publishing schedule, no marketing department, and no distributors or wholesalers. Books will be for sale only through our offices in Livingston, Montana, by phone, fax, regular mail, e-mail, or online at our website. And they will be for sale only to individuals and independent booksellers, never to chains or other entities having a corporate orientation. This eliminates the practices of discounting and remaindering. And all sales will be final, with a strict no-return policy. For readings and signings we will consign books, thus protecting the stores. The motto of the press is "Quality and Integrity Without Compromise."

No distribution, no stores. It was lunacy, and it was a shame.

After Clark City closed again, Russell tried to concentrate on painting, and after deepening financial trouble and a struggle with the IRS, he spent more and more time in California. I last saw him at a memorial for my father in the fall of 2016, with Guy and Tom also at the same table, in a room of old friends. Russell died on November 10, 2019, in California. To quote Rick Bass, in a beautiful 2022 tribute published in *Anglers Journal*, "Russell Chatham's art was his life—there are still a few like this out there—but the much greater trick, his life was also his art. He had no filters to the world."

In editing this collection, I tried to select the best work of each writer that excerpted well and offered some variety. I would like to have taken more from *Silent Seasons*, but it wasn't originally a Clark City book, and so I stuck to pieces that explained Russell's world. Clark City books largely or entirely missing from this anthology include the most anomalous things we published, *Hua Hu Ching* by Brian Walker and the screenplay tie-in for *A River Runs Through It*, with a script by Richard Friedenberg and an essay by Robert Redford, the reissued Wolo books, and two good novels for which I was unable to track down permissions: *The Lady with the Alligator Purse* by Ernest Finney and *My Sister Gone* by Kathryn Marshall.

And another note: Almost all of Clark City's authors were men. I didn't feel good about it then, and I feel worse now (and am especially sad to have not been able to make contact with Kathryn Marshall's estate). Many of the authors slated for publication in future seasons and solicited by me or by Russell were women. Part of the failure had to do with who submitted manuscripts—we were overwhelmed by hunting and fishing books, which we almost entirely put to one side. In the second life of the press, Russell and Sally Epps started to rectify the problem, especially with the wonderful *Motherlode*.

—Jamie Harrison

Nonfiction

I **THINK I NEED TO QUALIFY** the "non" part of this category, at least for some of the following excerpts. Truth is one thing to Guy de la Valdène, at least on the topic of woodcock, or Rick Bass, writing about the return of wolves to the continental United States—their work is carefully observed, well reported, innately honest. For the rest, I'll lead with this story about Tom McGuane, from a *Sports Illustrated* letter from the publisher, circa 1971:[2]

> Down the dusty main street of Livingston, Mont. (pop. 6,783) one high noon not so long ago—or so the story is told—marched grimly the man whose byline appears on page 40 of this issue of SI. He was holding a gun squarely in the back of another of our occasional contributors: Jim Harrison, poet, author and thoroughly convincing Western bandit. Spotting a tourist, our first author thrust the gun into his hand with the harsh command: "Keep this man covered while I get the sheriff," and disappeared around the corner. At which point our second author took off in the opposite direction, leaving the poor dude with an unloaded gun, a reeling mind and no sheriff anywhere in sight.

* * *

2 For the record, Tom says *SI* got it wrong. It was his brother, Johnny McGuane, who held the gun on my father. I'm sure *SI* would regret its error. —Editor

THOMAS McGUANE

Tom McGuane (1939–), born in Wyandotte, Michigan, is a rancher and a fisherman, a Stegner Fellow, a Yale School of Drama graduate, a National Book Award nominee, and a cutting-horse champion. His ten novels include *The Sporting Club*, *Ninety-two in the Shade*, *Nobody's Angel*, and *The Cadence of Grass*; nonfiction collections include *An Outside Chance* and *Some Horses*. Lately, with some relief, he's concentrated on short stories (the collections *To Skin a Cat*, *Gallatin Canyon*, *Crow Fair*, and *Cloudbursts*), many of which have first appeared in *The New Yorker*.

No one writes a better sentence, and no one is funnier. In my childhood, his visits were filled with lost dogs and roars and shrieks of laughter. In a recent email, a day in Florida was made up of "foul low skies, dirty water, wind, morons."

This first essay, a more truthful introduction to Russell's world than anything I could write, appeared in *Russell Chatham* (first published by Winn Books in 1984, reprinted by CCP in 1987); the second appeared in *Sports Illustrated* in 1971 and was reprinted in *Silent Seasons* (Lyons 1978, CCP 1988).

Chatham v. the Facts

from *Russell Chatham*, 1987
by Thomas McGuane

BECAUSE WE LIVE in flyover country, we try to figure out what is going on elsewhere by subscribing to magazines. Recently I was surprised to see, in a famous art publication, great attention directed to paintings of innumerable pastel beans. Another page displayed a huge shadowless lozenge. A passionate column explained colored space units to me once and for all.

The only painter I know very well is one of my best friends, and he lives up at the top of the creek upon which my ranch is located. I own a number of his paintings. Most of them are landscapes, powerful evocations of Montana, full of light, shapes, and ideas ruled by the most dignified style. His name is Russell Chatham.

I thought of Russ as I read about the pastel bean paintings. Frankly, the shadowless lozenge troubled me more than the others. I felt it was keeping customers of art from buying my friend's paintings, and, moreover, relegating him to life on the barter system when the rest of the world danced merrily to cash register tunes and credit rumbas. Why was Russ being singled out? Why was that lozenge after him?

One thing that might be considered is that the habit of trading still exists in Montana. Whether this is a vestige of the Old West, the Depression, or a reflection of limited job opportunities, I couldn't say. But ranchers couldn't operate on their limited (usually one-family) work forces if they couldn't trade services and commodities—meat for hay, wire for water, a rifle for a TV, horsebreaking for truck repairs. Montana's bartering habits are such that when mate-swapping finally arrives, it should have a vigorous future—a wife for a drum of diesel, a husband for a crossbow or a gerbil exercise wheel.

I recently traded a riverboat, a trailer, and a pair of oars for a small oil. Chatham plans to take the boat to British Columbia behind one of his five cars, an incredible ghost fleet of mufflerless low-riders that will prowl the golden river bottoms of Montana in search of mothballs. Inside, the painter balances a can of Great Falls Select and tries to figure how to get money out of the flying bean people. Only today he has read glowing notices of a show in Berkeley featuring unpainted canvases. Our man is hot around the collar. The headwaters of the Missouri seem to pour into his red, angry eyes. He tilts the can until he can no longer see the hood of his speeding derelict.

As I see it, current orthodoxy has it that a painting that you can describe is faulty, inherently so. There is a body of heretics, the superrealists, for instance, attempting COMPLETELY describable paintings. Modernism has grown naughty. The last residue of the high-priest fools of earlier in the century is the attitude that the viewer knows either nothing of a painting's meaning or only and exactly what he is ordered to know. The viewer is the fish perpetually shot in the barrel.

But before I expose myself to a vigorous demand for my credentials, let us have a look at how a serious painter survives, year after year, in Livingston, Montana, a railroad and cattle town with a few banks and a dozen or so bars.

First of all, the bars are there to help us with the long winters and unpleasant reviews. The Wrangler Bar on West Park, facing the tremendous old railroad station, is a good place to look for Chatham. He has one blind eye and a nose too crooked to line up a shot with at the pool table. However, he slamshoots eight ball of a winter's evening, walking around the table with a two-piece stick and moving his drink only to make a shot. He wears a huge snot-green sweater that you might associate with the kind of people who rob lobster pots or who drive unheated taxis in Vancouver, pointing out Chinamen to tourists. Bob Burns owns this bar. He is a generous and charming man who, with his family, owns eleven Chatham paintings. Mary Beth Burns, a daughter, won one shooting pool. The others were gifts; but we cannot rule out bar tabs and the specter of bartering.

When I decided to go around the area to look at some of the paintings Chatham had done over the last decade, I thought first of my neighbors

Wilbur and Dorotha Lambert. They have been here all their lives and typify a minority of extremely hardworking farmer-ranchers, contemptuous of the cowboy myth.

When I got to the Lamberts', Wilbur had been digging some gravel for one of his projects and found an old Indian dinner party—a young buffalo's skeleton, charred bones cracked for their marrow, and a neatly cleaved skull. There were bits of obsidian scattered with the bones.

We went inside and looked at the paintings; one was a mysterious little grassy landscape with a rather expressionist sheep evaporating in the middle.

Wilbur said, "It's just like when you come across the cow pass. Up close it don't look like nothin'. But you stand back and it's so natural-like."

Dorotha called from the kitchen, saying, "My dough is rising. I'm not ignoring you, but my husband don't like boughten bread."

"What do you think of Russ's painting?" I asked her.

"It's so different. I love it. It's just him."

"What'd you give for this one?" I asked.

"A load of firewood and an armful of smoked whitefish."

On the far wall was an uncanny portrait of Wilbur in hard sunlight, with the ruination of a hat he wears while irrigating. That was exchanged for babysitting with Russ's daughter, clothing repairs, and zucchini. They liked Chatham because "he don't have no airs and he don't go telling you how you should do it."

Wilbur added, "He's the only man in the country who never drives the same car two times in a row. Them cars is so bad they have to be rested. He's the only man in the country who redoes his plumbing every year. When you're headed south, there's no time to drain the pipes."

Next I went to see John Fryer, who runs Sax & Fryer, a family store that has been in Livingston since the 1880s. It's where you go for a cigar, a friend's book, school supplies, trout flies, or a state flag. Like Sixth Street Conoco on the corner of Park or the Pastime Bar off Callender Street, it is one of those beautifully run small businesses that are among the last perquisites of small-town living. Recently, we lost our counter checks—a bad sign.

John and I went to the N.P. Connection to drink a beer and ordered margaritas. "I've got two paintings," said John. "One is a small oil. It was a gift from Russ. It was kind of a Christmas card one year. Then I've got a marsh scene I bought at a Ducks Unlimited auction. I was bidding against the First National Park Bank. I loved the painting, but I wanted to head off a situation where they could say they already had one. They really should buy one of his big ones." [*They did. R.C.*]

Of the banks in Livingston only one owns a Chatham. Banks in the West tend to commission sentimental western extravaganzas for their walls—cowboys, Indians, and cavalrymen to hang over the secretaries' heads and the tellers' cages.

John Fryer said, "Chatham takes us away from the Kodachrome spectrum we were raised on. He saves us from the world of Smirnoff's ads."

Nevertheless, I wish his grave and deeply understood reflections on our beautiful region hung in our institutions. But Livingston is now arriving at that level of sophistication where a thirty-foot welded dog turd lying on the city hall lawn would seem like just the thing to a lot of people.

I was sitting in William Hjortsberg's house at Pine Creek. He is the son of a Scandinavian immigrant and the author of cool and often terrifying works of fiction. He is a Chatham owner. The first thing he bought was a sketch. "I was drunk when I bought it," he explained. At the time, the sketch seemed to contain all the world's happiness in a portable version. Sober, he paid for it in four installments. He also owns a mysterious, nearly monochromatic winter landscape with a single smokelike yellow aspen, odder than the most pastel flying bean.

"Almost my earliest acquaintance with Russ Chatham," Hjortsberg recalled, "I was staying at your place in Key West. A man came to the door looking for Chatham. I thought it was an insurance salesman. It was the FBI. I heard Prokofiev in my mind. I saw J. Edgar Hoover, I called Russ. He was staying in Nicasio, California, at a fraternal organization called Druids Hall. Someone had circulated a seditious newsletter from his address. Chatham kept writing the FBI to explain, and they kept arriving after he'd gone somewhere else."

Hjortsberg indicated his large Chatham oil, a Yellowstone landscape. "It's against the wrong wall," he complained, "but it's the only place it can go. I bought a light for it from Brookstone's Hard-to-Find Tools catalog, but it just made a splotch on it. You have to wait for winter. Then the leaves fall and light comes through the windows; that's when you have to see it."

I felt his intense pride in having it, the same thing I got from others in the Chatham barter zone.

Joe Swindlehurst, a Livingston attorney, bought a painting at an auction in precisely the circumstances that New York, Los Angeles, Santa Fe, and Scottsdale gallery people would find contemptible and hilarious. The auction was held around the swimming pool at a local motel.[3]

Chatham priced this painting and asked Swindlehurst to bid it up to a certain figure. Things got out of control, and Swindlehurst ended up paying twice the amount they'd been hoping for. Chatham winked at him and said, "Don't worry. You'll send your kids to college on it."

Swindlehurst said, "I'm embarrassed because I paid too little." This time, Chatham had come away with money and not a set of Swedish aircraft wrenches or portable kennels.

Mike Art of Pray, Montana, traded lifetime swimming privileges at Chico Hot Springs for a painting. Chatham swims less than he should, given that he is around forty and has rarely had really thorough medical exams. Which brings us to his doctor, one Dennis Noteboom, a Dakotan, a former all-state basketball player; in all respects, a sport and a gentleman.

The sport here is an obscure one. Noteboom ran horses for three summers on Chatham's pasture. He did not charge Chatham for medical services. Then Noteboom bought a painting for three times what Chatham was asking, while insisting that that was half its worth. Next, the Dakotan traded an airplane ticket to San Francisco for a small painting and guide service in that city. Chatham was an excellent guide in every way but one: He sought to provide a duck dinner and headed out with his shotgun. As there were no ducks available, he shot and prepared numerous blackbirds.

The shotgun employed by Chatham was acquired in a deal with the sharp Montana trader Harmon Henkin. I called Henkin about the matter.

Henkin said, "It was a Model Twelve, Winchester, sixteen-gauge."

"Field grade?" I asked.

"Medium grade, I'd say."

"Did it have a ventilated rib?" (There's no such thing as "medium grade.")

---

3 At another auction around this same pool, the only painting that sold had a moon. On the second day of the auction, several landscapes featured still drying moons. — Editor

"I would not so state for publication," said Henkin.

"How did you find trading with Chatham?"

"No hard bargaining," said Henkin. "Chatham panics and goes limp. It's like a Chihuahua facing a Saint Bernard."

"What sort of painting was it?"

"A small early landscape."

"Any other trades?"

"Yes," said Henkin. "I traded a fishing rod for a portrait. As they say on Santa Monica Boulevard, he wanted my pole badly."

"Are you happy with your deal?"

"I can live with it."

The young lady who is typing this, Carol Spalding of the Hookham & Lindeman real estate agency, traded an afghan for a painting. She has not completed the afghan. Chatham has not completed the painting. Both express continued belief in the barter.

Becky and Peter Fonda live in an old log home at the foot of a tall, sage-covered hill, popular with western diamondback rattlesnakes. Crossing the porch, range after range of Chatham raw material faces behind you. Opening the front door, the cool wooden interior is ruled by fifteen Chatham oils, perhaps the most wide-ranging collection of his work. The effect is amplified by the roar of children, the continuous smell of cooking, and the constantly ringing telephone. It is very different from the quiet air-conditioned rooms where the shadowless lozenge seems happiest.

Richard Brautigan disliked the view from one of his windows. It was the year the Indians confused him for Custer at Crow Agency. He had Chatham make a better view from that window. Chatham's recompense was a pig named Vivian. Vivian has since nourished Chatham.

Attorney Arnold Huppert, after a normal, grownup negotiation, arranged a cash deal with Chatham to do portraits of his four sons. By the time Chatham had done three, the fourth had moved to Portland. Chatham then portrayed Mrs. Huppert's dog. Both Hupperts were delighted, but Chatham would accept only ducks in payment for this last. Is he fatally drawn to barter? The Huppert was nearly an all-cash deal; the ducks appeared only at the end.

The local tale goes on. Morris Blakeley, cattleman, owns two paintings.

Terry Cousins, one (babysitting); Cindy Murphy, one (bartending); Dick Lamuth, one (accounting); Sandi Lee, four (ask her); David Colmey, two (veterinary services). And out of town, many others own Chathams, even a few nabobs. But we're just talking about Livingston, Montana.

I went up to the head of the creek to Chatham's house. The water in the stream is only a foot or so deep. Many decades ago, a depressed Englishman named Hall lived here. He used to threaten suicide periodically and leap into the shallows. Chatham had a similar moment sometime back. He burned twelve paintings. But he stayed out of the creek.

There is a stucco house, a log barn, a few old buildings, one of which has been converted into a studio. And there is the famous Chatham car garden.

I went inside. Chatham was dressed in his prison trustee's costume, playing Rickie Lee Jones and disconsolately regarding a kitchen remodeling that had stalled out. A barter could be at hand. There were, here and there, signs of Chatham's training as an artist—Ansel Adams's photograph of Chatham's grandfather, Gottardo Piazzoni, at work on one of the fourteen remarkable panels that hang in the San Francisco Public Library. In some ways, Piazzoni is a real precursor of his grandson. He was active from 1900 to 1945, and his circle included a curious grouping of such Californians as Adams, Arthur Putnam, and Imogen Cunningham.

A self-portrait of Maurice Del Mue, Chatham's uncle, hangs on the east wall. Del Mue was a commercial illustrator, and Chatham used to paint at his house. Del Mue designed the Arm & Hammer box and the Hills Bros. coffee can with the little yellow man drinking coffee. He was very successful and was married to a French model who spent all his money on defunct gold mines throughout the West and bankrupted him. Del Mue had tuberculosis when he was teaching Chatham to paint, and was living on dog food. He offered such advice as "Keep sitting on the ground like that and you'll get piles." When Chatham set up his easel for him, Del Mue would get too excited, suffer a tubercular attack, and have to lie down. Between Piazzoni and Del Mue, there was, in addition to a background of vision and draftsmanship, a notion that art was all family and friends.

Chatham's scheme for breaking out of the circle of barter on this particular day went as follows: A man in Los Angeles was very interested in an enormous painting. We would send the painting to Los Angeles in my pickup truck. Chatham would sell the painting for money, fill the pickup with California wine. Friends from the old barter days would split up the truckload of wine when it got back to Montana and share the travel expenses. Chatham found two unemployed nurses to make the drive.

It was with some sentiment, perhaps sadness, that we viewed the possibility that a major blow to our time-honored system of swapping was about to be delivered. Even Chatham's friends wondered if it was going to be coin of the realm from now on. But Chatham has to live amid the franchises with the rest of us. They don't take trade-ins at Chicken Delight, no matter how hungry you are. Maybe the same dread wind that blew the counter checks from our stores last year would get Chatham.

The painting arrived in Los Angeles, gliding into the geek metropolis on the back of my truck. The prospective buyer hated it. The nurses stayed two extra weeks in a heat wave. The wine turned to vinegar. When we sampled it, Russ raised somber eyes to mine and said, "What we need is an unsuspecting buyer."

I guess the lozenge got the truck.[4]

---

4 According to Dick Murphy, Russell's longtime framemaker and friend, the spoiled wine was doled out to drunks behind the gallery for several weeks.—Editor

Casting on a Sea of Memories

from *Silent Seasons: Twenty-One Fishing Stories*, 1988
by Thomas McGuane

BECAUSE THIS WAS A VISIT and a return, I might have had the nerve, right at the beginning, to call it *Sakonnet Point Revisited* and take my lumps on the Victorianism and sentimentality counts, though half a page of murder and sex at the end would bail that out. But one always knew from Lit I on that if you are to cultivate a universal irony, as Edmund Wilson told Scott Fitzgerald to do, you must never visit anything in your works, much less revisit—ever.

But when you go back to a place where you spent many hours of childhood, you find that some of it has become important, if not actually numinous, and that Lit I might just have to eat hot lead for the moment, because there is no way of suppressing that importance. Also, there is the fact of its being no secret anyway. A Midwestern childhood is going to show, for instance, even after you have retired from the ad agency and are a simple crab fisherman by the sea, grave with Winslow Homer marineland wisdom. Sooner or later someone looks into your eyes and sees a flash of corn and automobiles, possibly even the chemical plant at Wyandotte, Michigan. You can't hide it.

Still, there was one thing certainly to be avoided: to wit, when you go back to the summer place everything seems so small.

You protest: "But when I got there, everything *did* seem small . . ."

Don't say it! The smallness of that which is revisited is one of the touchstones of an egregious underground literature in which the heart is constantly wrung by the artifacts of childhood.

Students of Lit I: concentrate on all that dreck on the beach that didn't used to be there, won't you? Get the usual garbage, but lay in there for the real nonbiodegradables, too. This is 1978: be sure the aluminum cans and the polystyrene crud show up on the page. The great thing, ironists, is the stuff is really there! So, questions of falsification and literary decorum are both answered satisfactorily.

I had neared Sakonnet Point thinking, "This place is loaded with pitfalls," and I had visualized a perfect beach of distant memory now glittering with mercury, oiled ducks, aluminum and maybe one defunct but glowing nuclear submarine. And I met my expectations at my first meal in the area: the Down East Clam Special. The cook's budget had evidently been diverted into the tourist effluvium inspired by the American Revolution that I saw in the lobby. The clams that were in my chowder and fritters and fried clams were mere shadows of their former selves, in some instances calling into question whether they had ever been clams at all.

On my plate was Lit I, in parable form, come to haunt me. I knew at that moment that I had my imaginative sights. As a result, I actually returned to Sakonnet Point half thinking to see the whalers of the *Pequod* striding up from their dories to welcome me. And, truly, when I saw the old houses on the rocky peninsula, they fitted the spangled Atlantic around them at exactly the equipoise that seems one of the harmonics of childhood.

I had my bass rod in the car and drove straight to Warren's Point. There was a nice shore-break surf and plenty of boiling white water that I could reach with a plug. Nevertheless, I didn't rush it. I needed a little breakthrough to make the pursuit plausible. When you are fishing on foot, you have none of the reassurances that the big accouterments of the sport offer. No one riding a fighting chair on a hundred-thousand-dollar John Rybovich sport-fisherman thinks about *not getting one* in quite the same terms as the man on foot.

Before I began, I could see on the horizon the spectator boats from the last day of the America's Cup heading home. The Goodyear blimp seemed as stately in the pale sky as the striped bass I had visualized as my evening's reward.

I began to cast, dropping the big surface plug, an Atom Popper, into the white water around boulders and into the tumbling backwash of waves. I watched the boats heading home and wondered if *Gretel* had managed a comeback. During the day I had learned that an old friend of the family was in Fall River recovering from a heart attack and that his lobster pots still lay inside the course of the cup race. I wondered about that and cast until I began to have those first insidious notions that I had miscalculated the situation.

But suddenly, right in front of me, bait was in the air and the striped green-and-black backs of bass coursed through it. It is hard to convey this surprise: bait breaking like a small rainstorm and, bolting through the frantic minnows, perhaps a dozen striped bass. They went down at the moment I made my cast and reappeared thirty feet away. I picked up and cast again, and the same thing happened. Then the fish vanished.

I had blown the chance by not calculating an interception. I stood on my rock and rather forlornly hoped it would happen again. To my immediate right baitfish were splashing out of the water, throwing themselves up against the side of a sea-washed boulder. It occurred to me, slowly, that they were not doing this out of their own personal sense of sport. So I lobbed my plug over, made one turn on the handle, hooked a striper and was tight to the fish in a magical burst of spray. The bass raced around among the rocks and seaweed, made one dogged run toward open water, then came my way. When he was twenty feet from me, I let him hang in the trough until another wave formed. I glided the fish in on it and beached him.

The ocean swells and flattens, stripes itself abstractly with foam and changes color under the clouds. Sometimes a dense flock of gulls hangs overhead and their snowy shadows sink into the green translucent sea.

Standing on a boulder amid breaking surf that is forming offshore, accelerating and rolling toward you, is, after a while, like looking into a fire. It is mesmeric.

All the while I was here I thought of my Uncle Bill, who had died the previous year and in whose Sakonnet house I was staying, as I had in the past. He was a man of some considerable local fame as a gentleman and a wit. And he had a confidence and a sense of moral precision that amounted, for some people, to a mild form of tyranny. But for me, his probity was based almost more on his comic sense than his morality—though the latter was considerable.

He was a judge in Massachusetts. I have heard that in his court one day two college students were convicted of having performed a panty raid on a girls' dormitory. My uncle sentenced them to take his charge card to Filene's department store in Boston and there "to exhaust their interest in ladies' underwear."

He exacted terrific cautions of my cousin Fred, my brother John and me and would never, when I fished here as a boy, have allowed me to get out on the exposed rocks I fished from now. His son Fred and I were not allowed to swim unguarded, carry pocketknives or go to any potentially dangerous promontory to fish, which restriction eliminated all the good places.

And he had small blindnesses that may have been infuriating to his family, for all I know. To me, they simply made him more singular. By today's or even the standards of that day, he was rather unreconstructed, but this makes of him an infinitely more palpable individual in my memory than the adaptable nullities who have replaced men like him.

His discomfiture will be perceived in the following: he invited Fred and me to his court in Fall River. To his horrified surprise, the first case before him was that of a 300-pound lady, the star of an all-night episode of *le sexe multiple*, and included a parade of abashed sailors who passed before Fred's and my astounded eyes at the behest of the prosecution. Unreconstructed in her own way, the lady greeted the sailors with a heartiness they could not return.

After the session closed for the day, my uncle spirited us to Sakonnet to think upon the verities of nature. For us, at the time, nature was largely striped bass and how to get them. But the verity of a fat lady and eleven sailors trapped in the bell jar of my Uncle Bill's court fought for our attention on equal footing.

I hooked another bass at the end of a long cast. Handsome: you see them blast a plug out at the end of your best throw. I landed the fish as the sun fell.

I was here during the hurricane that made the surf break in the horse pasture across the road from the house. Shingles lifted slowly from the garage roof and exploded into the sky. The house became an airplane; unimaginable plants and objects shot past its windows. The surf took out farm fences and drove pirouettes of foam into the sky. My cousins and I treated it as an adventure. Uncle Bill was our guarantee against the utter feasibility of the house going underwater. And if it flooded, we knew he would bring a suitable boat to an upstairs window.

Late that day the hurricane was over, having produced delirium and chaos: lobster pots in the streets, commercial fishing boats splintered all over the rocks, yards denuded of trees and bushes, vegetation burned and killed by wind-driven salt water.

My cousin Fred and I stole out and headed for the shore, titillated by looting stories. The rocky beach was better than we dreamed; burst tackle chests with more bass plugs than we could use, swordfish harpoons, ship-to-shore radios, marine engines, the works.

Picking through this lovely rubble like a pair of crows, we were approached by the special kind of histrionic New England lady (not Irish Catholic like us, we knew) who has got a lot of change tied up in antiques and family *objets* that point to her great familial depth in this part of the world. She took one look at us and called us "vile little ghouls," which rather queered it for us, neither of us knowing what ghouls were.

I kept fishing after dark, standing on a single rock and feeling disoriented by the foam swirling around me. I was getting sore from casting and jigging the plug. Moreover, casting in the dark is like smoking in the dark; something is missing. You don't see the trajectory or the splash. You don't see the surface plug spouting and spoiling for trouble. But shortly I hooked a fish. It moved very little. I began to think it was possibly a deadhead rolling in the wash. I waited, just trying to keep everything together. The steady, unexcited quality of its movement began to convince me that it was not a fish. I lifted the rod sharply to see if I could elicit some more characteristic movement. And I got it. The fish burned off fifty or sixty yards, sulked, let me get half of it back and did the same again.

I began to compose the headline: LUNKEROONY FALLS TO OUT-OF-STATE BASSMASTER. "'I clobber them big with my top-secret technique,' claims angler-flaneur Tom McGuane of Livingston, Mont.," etc., etc.

The bass began to run again, not fast or hysterical but with the solid, irresistible motion of a Euclid bulldozer easing itself into a phosphate mine. It mixed up its plays, bulling, running, stopping, shaking. And then it was gone.

When I reeled up, I was surprised that I still had the plug, though its hooks were mangled beyond use. I had been cleaned out. Nevertheless, with two good bass for the night, I felt resigned to my loss. No I didn't.

I took two more bass the next day. There was a powerful sense of activity on the shore. Pollock were chasing minnows right up against the beach. And at one sublime moment at sundown, tuna were assailing the bait, dozens of the powerful fish in the air at once, trying to nail the smaller fish from above.

Then it was over and quiet. I looked out to sea in the last light, the white rollers coming in around me. The clearest item of civilization from my perspective was a small tanker heading north. Offshore, a few rocky shoals boiled whitely. The air was chilly. It looked lonely and cold.

But from behind me came intimate noises: the door of a house closing, voices, a lawn mower. And, to a great extent, this is the character of bass fishing from the beach. In very civilized times it is reassuring to know that wild fish will run so close that a man on foot and within earshot of lawn mowers can touch their wildness with a fishing rod.

I hooked a bass after dark, blind-casting in the surf, a good fish that presented some landing difficulties; there were numerous rocks in front of me, hard to see in the dark. I held the flashlight in my mouth, shining it first along the curve of rod out to the line and to the spot among the rocks where the line met the water, foaming very bright in the light. The surf was heavier now, booming into the boulders around me.

In a few moments I could see the thrashing bass, the plug in its mouth, a good fish. It looked radically striped and impressive in the backwash.

I guided the tired striper through the rocks, beached him, removed the plug and put him gently into a protected pool. He righted himself and I watched him breathe and fin, more vivid in my light beam than in any aquarium. Then abruptly he shot back into the foam and out to sea. I walked into the surf again, looking for the position, the exact placement of feet and tension of rod while casting that had produced the strike.

One of the earliest trips to Sakonnet included a tour of The Breakers, the Vanderbilt summer palazzo. My grandmother was with us. Before raising her large family she had been among the child labor force in the Fall River mills, the kind of person who had helped make really fun things like palazzos at Newport possible.

Safe on first by two generations, I darted around the lugubrious mound, determined to live like that one day. Over the fireplace was an agate only slightly smaller than a fire hydrant. It was here that I would evaluate the preparation of the bass I had taken under the cliffs by the severest methods: eleven-foot Calcutta casting rod and handmade block-tin squid. The bass was to be brought in by the fireplace, *garni*, don't you know; and there would be days when the noble fish was to be consumed in bed. Many, many comic books would be spread about on the counterpane.

We went on to Sakonnet. As we drove I viewed every empty corn or potato field as a possible site for the mansion. The Rolls Silver Ghost would be parked to one side, its leather back seat slimy from loading stripers.

The sun came up on a crystalline fall day; blue sky and delicate glaze. I hiked down the point beach, along the red ridge of rock, the dense beach scrub with its underledge of absolute shadow. As I walked I drove speeding clusters of sanderlings before me. If I did not watch myself, there would be the problem of sentiment.

When I got to the end and could see the islands with their ruins, I could observe the narrow, glittering tidal rip like an oceanic continuation of the rocky ridge of the point itself.

A few days before, the water had been cloudy and full of kelp and weed, especially the puffs of iodine-colored stuff that clung tenaciously to my plug. Today, though, the water was clear and green, with waves rising translucent before whitening onto the hard beach. I stuck the butt of my rod into the sand and sat down. From here, beautiful houses could be seen along the headlands. A small farm ran down the knolls with black-and-white cattle grazing along its tilts. An American spy was killed by the British in the farm's driveway.

My cousin Fred came that evening from Fall River and we fished. The surf was heavier and I hooked and lost a fish very early on. There were other bass fishermen out, bad ones mostly. They trudged up and down the shore with their new rods, not casting but waiting for an irresistible sign to begin.

When it was dark, Fred, who had waded out to a far rock and who periodically vanished from my view in the spray, hooked a fine bass. After some time, he landed it and made his way through the breakers with the fish in one hand, the rod in the other.

On my previous nights I had gotten a fish on my last cast of the evening. I made one more tonight and got nothing. I kept casting, hoping to take a bass on my last cast. Nothing. And my time had almost run out.

It is assumed that the salient events of childhood are inordinate. During one of my first trips to Sakonnet, a trap boat caught an enormous oceanic sunfish, many hundred pounds in weight. A waterfront entrepreneur who usually sold crabs and tarred handlines bought the sunfish and towed it to the beach in an enclosed wooden wagon where he charged ten cents admission to see it. I was an early sucker—and a repeater. In some primordial way the sight seems to have taken like a vaccination; I remember very clearly ascending the wooden steps into the wagon whose windows let water-reflected light play over the ceiling.

One by one we children goggled past the enormous animal laid out on a field of ice. The huge lolling discus of the temperate and tropical seas met our stares with a cold eye that was not less soulful for being the size of a hubcap.

Many years later I went back to Sakonnet on a December afternoon as a specific against the torpor of school. I was walking along the cove beach when I saw the wagon, not in significantly worse repair than when I had paid to get in it. And, to be honest, I never made the connection that it was the same wagon until I stepped inside.

There on a dry iceless wooden table lay the skeleton of the ocean sunfish.

It seemed safe to conclude in the face of this utterly astounding occasion that I was to be haunted. Accommodating myself to the fish's reappearance, I adjusted to the unforeseeable in a final way. If I ever opened an elevator door and found that skeleton on its floor, I would step in without comment, finding room for my feet between ribs, and press the button of my destination.

At the end of a fishing trip you are inclined to summarize in your head. A tally is needed for the quick description you will be asked for: so many fish at such and such weights and the method employed. Inevitably, what actually happened is indescribable.

GUY DE LA VALDÈNE

Guy de la Valdène (1944–2023) came from a different world. He was born in New York while the Nazis were using the family's chateau for regional offices. His father was a French count, a World War I flying ace, and an engineer who served with the Free French during World War II in the Mediterranean; his mother was the sculptor and aviator Diana Guest, a cousin of Winston Churchill and an heir to the Phipps fortune.

But it was a high school friend who changed Guy's life. Gil Drake's father opened a bonefishing lodge on Grand Bahama Island called Deep Water Cay, and both boys spent months every year fishing during their teens. They never stopped. By the time Guy was introduced to Tom McGuane in 1969, they both knew what they were doing.

Guy came to our house in Michigan for the first time in the fall of 1972, and he (and Russell too) continued to visit during hunting season for over two decades, staying—at least until my father bought a cabin in Grand Marais, Michigan—for two to three weeks. It was a delirium of food and wine and talk, other drugs and wet dogs, birds dangling from the porch and feathers everywhere in the yard. I loved it. Guy was an incredibly good cook. My mother was no slouch, but Guy and Russell's visits upped the ante. Woodcock and ruffed grouse; caviar and foie gras. We made screamingly hot Szechuan and perfect dumplings. I plucked, made desserts, rolled my first pasta.

Guy taught me how to eat, taught me how to drink, tried to give me an attitude I hadn't been born to, fibbed on my behalf to my parents when I stayed out too late. Later, when I'd first arrived in New York and was jobless, he paid me for woodcock research. I thought it was logical to trot up to the Morgan Library, with absolutely nothing by way of academic credentials but a BA, and try to translate eighteenth-century French hunting texts. Six years later, at Clark City, I wanted *Making Game* to be as beautiful on the page as it would have been read out loud. His other works are *The Fragrance of Grass*, *On the Water*, and *Red Stag*. He'd hoped to write about his father and was working on a book about the Atchafalaya Basin.

from

Making Game: An Essay on Woodcock

by Guy de la Valdène, 1990

I'VE ALWAYS ASSUMED that all birds mated and were born in the spring. I suppose I wanted it to be that way. I was wrong, but I still choose to believe that life—all life—hatches from womb or egg in May. It's a fine month, and it's simpler to think of it that way.

Because atmospheric conditions vary, it is difficult to pinpoint the exact date that spring begins for the woodcock. It may be as early as February in the mid-Northern states and as late as the second week in April in Ontario and Quebec. One thing is certain, however—spring begins for the males the moment they arrive on the breeding grounds. Cleverly waiting for good weather and for their prospective mates to work out their territorial differences, the females arrive a week or two later.

Spring confuses the males constantly. Although they winter in the South, the birds are opportunistic by nature and are content, as long as the earth remains soft, to stay just ahead of the weather. A freeze urges them farther and farther down the continent until, as in the case of Louisiana, land gives way to water. Mild winters, on the other hand, upset their metabolism, prompting a premature swelling of the males' testes and an irrational urge to fly north and be the first to claim a piece of real estate. Often those urges spell disaster. If the breeding grounds are frozen, there will be little if any food available. Some will die, a few will turn back, and still others will make do, feeding as best they can alongside riverbeds and creek bottoms. The urge to mate takes its toll on every species.

Woodcock appear portly. I observed one years ago, strutting across a sandy two-track, chest thrust outward, tail fanned, bobbing lasciviously up and down like a bullfrog, and I expected him to pitch over and impale his bill in the ground. I'm told that this behavior is a sign of nervousness, but in his case it was certainly disguised with élan.

In hand, the bird is a delight. From the crown of his head to the tip of his tail, he fits as if he'd been born to be palmed. Gauguin might well have painted him, cupped as an offering in the hands of a girl.

He is born with a long, thin bill designed for probing. This bill, which at first glance appears ungainly, is a wonder of engineering. Averaging two-and-three-quarters inches in length, it is a delicate organ, combining taste, touch and smell. The tip, which is slightly bulbous and overlaps the lower mandible, holds a miasma of delicate blood vessels and nerve endings that act as underground antennae in the detection of worms. A woodcock is born with a prehensile bill; a specific bone and musculature permits him to open the anterior third of his upper mandible, push dirt aside and seize his prey. The bird grasps and extracts worms between his tongue and the underside of his upper bill, both of which are as rough as sharkskin.

His nostrils are set high against his skull, presumably to enable him to feed without pressing upon his nasal cavities. His ears, instead of framing both sides of his head, are situated in front of and a bit beneath his eyes. The eyes in turn are proportionately larger than most birds' and set very high and to the rear of his skull. His sight is acute, and his range includes lateral, posterior and overhead vision. His eyes are also black and limpid, not eyes to dwell on if one intends to keep hunting. Over the millennia, while the woodcock's bill grew and his legs shortened, his eyes travelled backwards, forcing his brain to rotate on its axis to a unique upside-down position. This linear progression of sensory organs indicates that much of his skull is geared to the task of feeding.

When I started this book, the accepted Latin name for the American woodcock was *Philohela minor*, which translates into "little lover of the bogs." A year later the taxonomists changed the name back to *Scolopax minor*. Since 1788 the bird has been assigned no fewer than ten different names.

The American woodcock is related to one of six families of shorebirds. His is the family of *Scolopacidae*, which includes willets, curlews, sandpipers, plovers and others. In his case, although evolution urged him to the woods, like his cousin the snipe he retained his ancestral habits of probing and thus was rewarded with a long list of sobriquets that I won't dwell on except for one, and only because it applies to a subspecies I find offensive. Years ago it was believed that woodcock fed by sucking mud through their bills, and therefore in certain regions they were given the name of "bog suckers." An insulting assertion, but one that does deserve its place on the brass mastheads of most environmental agencies.

The woodcock's plumage deserves special attention. Overall, it is not unlike the color of a freshly killed brown trout or the skin of certain reptiles; a glance at a certain seventeenth-century Flemish canvas also reminds me of the subtle beauty that exudes from this relic of another age, whose survival depends on camouflage. Both male and female birds have identical coloration, and, except in youth or during a molt, the design remains constant throughout the seasons. The feathers, woven like bracelets on an artichoke, at times blend together and at other times are notched, barred, edged and tipped in an incredibly specific and purposeful kaleidoscope of patterns.

Woodcock sport a cream-colored jabot around the throat and a cinnamon tea apron over breast and abdomen. A sweeping black stroke runs from the bill, surrounds the eyes and tapers close to the occiput, next to four lateral ochre crossbars that sit above a Payne-grey forehead. A second but smaller signature appears lower on the cheek, darkly encasing his ears.

The base of the neck and back is mottled in burnt umber and black, except for four lines of slate grey. Two of those lines run from either side of the neck, forming two sides of a triangle ending at the cant of the back, while the others hug a straight line to the base of the wing. Paintings of the bird in flight and from the rear usually depict him lightly stamped with the letter "M." The base of the tail feathers is warm grey, giving way to mottled raw sienna tipped with black. The underpart, particularly visible when the bird fans, displays a prismatic sheen tinged in white-cream. The wings are mottled silver-grey to burnt umber near the body cavity and slowly darken to a uniform brown at the tips. A thin line of slate bisects the entirety of the wings to the primaries, while the upper part of the leg is covered in fine auburn down.

Everyone's perceptions of colors differ and vary with respect to light and taste. Some find woodcock dull compared to other species. I find that bruised peaches, reflections on gravel creeks, and the whip of red foxes evoke their memory. But then so does Pan.

RUSSELL CHATHAM

Russell Chatham (1939–2019) was a translator of light, a benevolent chaos agent, a man who ate not wisely but well, a man who (in Tom McGuane's affectionate words) "ruined his life with sport."

If you knew Russell, there was a good chance he changed your life, but there was reciprocity among his oldest friends: He may have begun writing because he loved to fish and wanted people to understand; he certainly continued writing because of the encouragement of his friends. "I don't have any illusions about the immortality of my prose," he wrote in the preface to *Dark Waters*, "but I do believe it hasn't hurt anyone." He would never have said such a thing about his painting: He was sure of his talent, and he was right.

A note on Russell's food essays: In 1984 or 1985, I flew out to Los Angeles to visit a friend and took the train up to San Francisco, where Russell was living with Suzanne Porter, who would become his third wife. Russell picked me up at the station, and we headed out to an Italian restaurant. I blearily recall rabbit and a long rant about his desire to import a bronze extruder to make pasta. The next day, while Suzanne worked to pay the rent, Russell took me to his favorite dim sum restaurant, where we split thirty-two dishes, with accompanying beverages. On to the Legion of Honor, where we saw his grandfather's work, and the casting pools at Golden Gate Park, where I vomited and napped under some shrubbery while Russell kept working the pool. On to dinner—I remember a capon, but where?—and a third day, which is hazy, but included Bolinas and another lunch and another dinner. It was the last time I actually ran for a plane across a tarmac (drunk again).

Hard as a Rock

from *The Angler's Coast*, 1990
by Russell Chatham

AS IS OFTEN THE CASE during summer, the northern California coast was fogbound. From the vast windows of the house where I was staying I couldn't see across the inlet to where Mendocino inhabited its mesa, a town so patently picturesque it was almost a relief not to be able to see it.

I was an anonymous painter behind plate glass. This was important because Mendocino is one of the artiest art colonies on the coast. There could be guilt by association: the county was dark with arts and crafts, decorated Volkswagen buses, inept pottery, much macramé, and embarrassing paintings. I was here to go fishing. My friends Harry and Charlie had just gotten back from an afternoon of gathering mussels and abalone. Charlie, a writer, considered it imperative that a part of each day be spent trying to catch *something*. Since there would be three of us going rockfishing the next day, Charlie was careful to save the abalone guts for bait. "I won't need any," I said. "I'm going to use flies."

Charlie scanned me for signs of brain damage. Without resolving the question, he put all the guts into a big plastic bag.

"We're going to need lots of bait!" he stated, with a concerned glance at me.

Charlie was not an early riser so Harry and I amused ourselves throughout the morning. Harry was a sculptor and an exhibition of his work was at one of the galleries; we went over to see it. The gallery was an old shed which had been white-washed inside and out. The lady who ran it had graying hair and wore faded blue jeans and a tasteful, handmade shawl. Both were standard issue.

"They never sell a damn thing," Harry remarked after we left. "Were you kidding?" he asked me.

"About what?"

"You can't use flies in the ocean, can you?"

"Sure, you'll see."

There was a certain broad headland where Harry and Charlie had permission to fish. It was a grassy meadow, with pine and cypress trees along its north side, ending abruptly at a rocky drop to the ocean. Fog hugged us closely, and the still air was damp and rich with sea smells.

Harry had a long bamboo pole with a short length of wire tied to the end of it. He was going "poke-poling": the pole with its short wire leader and baited hook is poked down into crevices in the rock. He intended to catch mostly eels and cabezon this way.

Charlie had an ordinary, stout fishing rod and a big Penn reel. He used Bull Durham bags filled with sand for sinkers because they didn't snag easily on the irregular bottom, and if he did lose one, it didn't matter because he had a lot more.

I had my fly rod; some concern was expressed over this. Charlie was anxious to arrange a wager before we began, and even renewed his offer of abalone guts. In truth, Charlie's interest in fishing was not entirely a matter of catching fish. This was partially due to the fact that he didn't catch many, but the real reason was that, for him, time spent fishing was time spent thinking. When he was sitting out there he turned over ideas, invented characters, built plots, and considered Beethoven's later string quartets. Inadvertently, I was going to ruin this for him.

"Catch many black snappers?" I asked.

"Once in a while. Wish I'd catch more."

"I'll get you a sackful," I promised with a smile.

Years ago I might have said "Ha!" In fact, I had said "Ha!" once about fifteen years ago. Luckily I hadn't said it aloud, and thus didn't have to eat it afterward. I was with Bill Schaadt careening up coastal Highway 1 in an old Plymouth, past Fort Ross to a place just south of Salt Point which he called the Rope Hole because it was so far down and so steep you had to climb down and up a rope to fish it.

Bill and I were just getting the hang of casting fly line with lead wire in it, which cut through the wash to where the fish were and was the main ingredient for successful rockfishing. We learned any kind of fly worked, including old steelhead flies, though it was easier just to tie an orange feather on a hook. That day we caught our limit of snappers, twenty apiece. I had cause to regret this on our way back up the rope. It was perhaps as close as I've ever come to cardiac arrest.

We did a great deal of fly-fishing for snappers after that. Once we launched a skiff from the mouth of the Russian River. We caught snappers all right, but were lucky to get back through the breakers. We fished at Salt Point, Fort Ross, and a hundred other nameless places in between. Later, I fished up and down the Oregon and Washington coasts. So I was a seasoned rockfisherman, a fact that Charlie hardly suspected.

Charlie was at a spot where a deep crevice cut back between two high slabs of rock. Here the surf surged in and out with mesmeric regularity, alternately revealing and hiding the bottom beneath lime-green foam. He caught an exotic rainbow perch on his first throw and was overly matter-of-fact about it.

"Bait?" he offered, with an upraised eyebrow.

Nearby, I found a deep hole ringed with kelp. Long casts are built into the lead line and with the help of an elevated position I dropped one about a hundred feet out. Charlie's eyes widened. He had never seen anything like it. He wondered no doubt what this painter, this, this . . . mere dauber was up to. He did not suspect that without even stepping lightly into a phone booth I—in the presence of catchable quarry—could rearrange my chromosomes into a facsimile of the mythical angler, Reeline Waderfly, who stopped at nothing in his neurotic quest for fish, and who was to sow the seeds of Charlie's imminent discontent. A three-pound snapper took the fly immediately. The next cast brought another one and so on until the burlap sack had been mercilessly filled. Meanwhile, Charlie sat hunched over his inert fishing rod.

When Harry rejoined us he was soaking wet and shivering. He had gotten out on a reef and a big roller had simply lifted him off, carried him out, then swept him back, depositing him again on the reef. He'd lost his sack of fish and had some pretty bad scrapes from sharp rock and mussels. It was time to go home.

Charlie was not the least bit glum. At the house he cheerfully assaulted a bottle of sauternes with a gleam in his eye which became a glaze at precisely the same rate the liquid's level dropped. I explained to him that the snappers liked to stay fairly high in the water, especially near kelp, and that he caught so few because his bait was on the bottom. I suggested he try a bobber but he wasn't listening. He reminded me of Mr. Toad seeing his first motor car.

"This is it," he said, "the miracle method!"

Sometime later I met Harry in San Francisco. He told me Charlie had gone up to Fort Bragg and bought a fly rod and reel on sale at one of the drugstores. He couldn't find any of that special line so he just got whatever they had.

"He's not the same," Harry went on. "He goes down every day and flails around on the rocks. There's no one to show him what to do and people think he's gone around the bend. Most of the time he's got his hook stuck in the kelp or on a rock or bush. Either that or in the seat of his pants. I think he can only throw it out about ten feet at best, which frustrates him so he comes home all on edge instead of soothed and relaxed like he used to. And he risks his life trying to get too far out on the reef because he knows he can't cast out to where the fish are. He doesn't even talk about Beethoven anymore."

"Has he caught anything?"

"Not yet."

Eating Around

from *Dark Waters: Essays, Stories and Articles*, 1988
by Russell Chatham

THREE PAIRS OF FEET dangle in the tepid water near the Marquesas, twenty miles off Key West. If your eyes wandered up past those ankles, shins, knees and thighs, you would soon see three oversized asses parked on the gunwale of an otherwise fast, sleek fishing skiff.

"Whose idea was it not to put the leftover dry-fried beef in the lunch?" Jim Harrison asks menacingly as he squints into the brutal June sun with his one good eye. He and Guy de la Valdène turn to look at me. "It was you, wasn't it? 'Oh, let's not put that in, it'll be too much out there in the heat. We have plenty with the Cuban sandwiches.' Well, let me tell you those sandwiches are a mere shadow of the ones we used to get. Christ, I mean they are *tiny*."

"Surely you can't hold me responsible for the Cuban-sandwich maker trying to please the town's major constituency."

"The dry-fried beef would have been nice to have," Guy says. "But we'll just go on in a little early and fix an hors d'oeuvre immediately. Now let's go try the North Face for a while."

The trim little skiff with its great burden moves slowly along the shore of the island. Guy is up on the platform in back, poling the boat along, Harrison is searching the horizon from the gunwale, sipping a rum and coke, and I am standing on the foredeck, fly rod in hand, waiting for the approach of tarpon. Sometimes these periods of poling, searching, and waiting can be excruciatingly long. It doesn't take much time for one's mind to drift to other topics, and one of the most persistent and interesting is always food.

For these purposes I'm glad we're not steelhead fishing in British Columbia. The fishing there is stupendous, but B.C. is no place to go for sophisticated cuisine, nor are the camps there suited to the do-it-yourselfer.

Now, your British Columbian loathes your French Canadian. In every way possible he considers the latter to be at best a horse's ass. Here people are in full reaction against "fancy food" (French), and in full support, though once removed, of clubfoot boiling and frying (English).

Half a dozen years ago, Michael Butler, Richard Brautigan, Guy and I found ourselves in Campbell River on Vancouver Island. With a gesture toward the water nearby, Brautigan offered to buy dinner. "Must be great seafood around here," he said.

We located what was described as "the best restaurant in town." No matter where you go there is one of these. There, we were favored with one of the most astonishing meals ever served. The details are lengthy, boring and disgusting, but the fresh-shrimp curry was a standout, a UFO based on Aunt Penny's white sauce, now somehow turned a dull gray. Curry flavor? Forget it. Mixed into this homemade quicksand was some rudely chopped celery, pimentos, and last and definitely least, a few tough canned shrimp, the largest of which would rest comfortably on a postage stamp. Entombed beneath it all was the rice, gelatinous and practically transparent.

"So much for fresh seafood," mumbled Brautigan.

It was in B.C. that I overhead one man advise another, "Don't eat breakfast in so-and-so's cafe. I ordered an omelette in there the other day and it was soft!" B.C. is one of the few places where they have puffy gray steaks that seem to have been simmered in water, fried eggs you can't slice with a razor blade and ravioli that are simply two piles of dough, with no filling, served in weak brown gravy. After eating for a while in western Canada you could compile an encyclopedia of bizarre and pointless foods, and have it illustrated by B. Kliban.

"What kind of hors d'oeuvre?" I ask without turning to address anyone in particular.

"What about fresh Szechuan noodles in sweet chili paste?"

"We ate all the noodles."

"We could get some stone-crab claws."

"Don't bore us. That's for a ladies' bridge club luncheon."

"Then you think of something."

"How about crispy pork dumplings? Or we could steam them. Better yet would be a bastardized mu shu pork where we double the ginger and garlic, add some chilis, and shoot some hot sesame oil in with the green onion and hoisin."

"That sounds good. Now, what can we have for dinner?"

"How about fresh yellowtail?"

"Fixed how?"

"Remember when we did it steamed over those veg . . . oh, shit!"

"What?"

"Son-of-a-bitch went right under the boat. Ninety, maybe a hundred pounds."

"Hmmm."

"Your turn to fish, Jim."

"You know," Jim says, gesturing with his cigarette, "we didn't come thousands of miles to go fishing just to have you not pay any attention and let all the fish swim under the boat. Get it? You have to look at the water or there's no point to any of this. Can't you think of anything except filling your big fat stomach?"

"I don't know, but there's a school of rollers heading our way and your fly line is all tangled around your feet."

"What! Jesus!"

"Just kidding. Wanted to see if you were paying attention after coming all these thousands of miles."

Guy's always calm voice interrupts. "Listen, Bubbleass and Needledick, we actually do have a string of fish coming in at about ten o'clock."

Harrison begins frantically pawing at the fly line. "C'mon now," he pleads hysterically. "Watch my line so it doesn't get hung up."

He makes his false casts with that sense of terror and urgency associated with fly fishing for tarpon, releasing the line only to have the headwind push it back into an unruly pile. Before he can recover, the tarpon have seen the boat and spook away, out of sight.

"Goddamn it." Jim moans with an absolutely sincere air of dejection.

The biggest difference between tarpon fishing with Jim and Guy in Key West during May, and bird hunting with them at Jim's home in Michigan during October (aside from the fact birds fly and fish swim, ha ha), is that while we never kill the tarpon, we most assuredly do kill the birds. We kill them not because we like to, but because you can't really prepare them for the table while they are still flying around.

The best part of Jim's house is the basement where the wine is. What could be finer than passing the time strolling among the bottles? The more superlative vintages are reserved for the more exotic meals, the ones to which guests are strictly excluded.

One of the most exquisite, if not the most exquisite meal of the entire fall, is one which Guy makes with woodcock: *salmis de bécasses à l'ancienne Christian Bourillot*. Guy not only makes the dish, he usually shoots the woodcock too, because Harrison misses them regularly, and as for myself, I may as well stay home trying to kill flies by slow pitching a softball at them.

The preparation of the salmis of woodcock involves not only sensitivity, but real knowledge of French cuisine. Of course, the woodcock will have been hung, undrawn and unplucked, for at least several days to develop and heighten their unique wild flavor. Roasting of the birds is done in a very hot oven for perhaps seven or eight minutes so the meat remains rare.

The sauce, which is enormously important, is made by browning the chopped carcasses in a *mirepoix* with butter, then flaming them with cognac, adding wine, and then combining the reduced liquid with a demi-glace. This is finally strained over the pieces of bird as they rest on croutons fried in butter and spread with intestines and foie gras. The heads are used as a garnish, the tiny brain considered a delicacy. When we are in line for this princely meal, the part of the cellar we look hardest at contains the old Margaux, Rothschilds, or Echézeaux.

"Let's look at the face of Ballast Key on our way in."

"I'll pole," I offer, "and Guy can fish for a change."

"You're not going to like it," Guy says with a twisted smile. "It's a hard bottom, it's deep and the swells from the Atlantic make it a real bitch just to balance on the platform let alone pole."

"Let Mr. Hotshot give it a try."

"Listen, I've poled here before. It's not that big of a deal."

Standing on the platform is a little like walking a tightrope, not that

I've ever walked one or ever will. But your feet and legs have to learn not to fight it, so you're not continually struggling for balance. Poling with the eighteen-foot fiberglass pole is not easy under the best of circumstances, and Guy was dead right when he described this spot.

I can't help but notice that my great weight is doing nothing to improve my poling technique and I wonder if there isn't a chance of obtaining some appreciable weight loss by devoting myself entirely to *nouvelle cuisine*. This passes through my mind only moments before the pole slips off the rocky bottom on a particularly difficult stroke, sending me straight into the ocean.

"Oh, for Christ's sake." Harrison rolls his eyes skyward, letting his arms hang exaggeratedly low at his sides.

"I think big boy needs a drink and some nourishment after all that poling."

"Yeah. And all that swimming."

A person who likes to eat and drink can really pull the plug in San Francisco. It has everything from the world's best hamburgers (at Clown Alley on Columbus), to the world's most esoteric and exotic foods (from, as they say, the four corners of the earth). And, as San Francisco is a very small city, your choice for the evening is never more than minutes away.

As big fans of the cooking of the Far East, where Marco Polo went to learn how to make spaghetti, Jim, Guy and I more often than not find ourselves in Chinatown, or close to it. Typically, we might go to the Great Eastern on Jackson Street, a place Brautigan showed us some years ago.

There, we might order sizzling rice soup, Mongolian lamb, asparagus beef, clams in black-bean sauce, snow peas with pork, almond pressed duck, fried prawns with plum sauce, sesame chicken, and usually three or four other vegetables or fish dishes depending on the season. We are often ridiculed by the otherwise dispassionate waiters.

Or we might try the Szechuan on Polk Street, where the Peking duck is as good as it gets. Given the time we would also hurt ourselves at Thai, Indonesian, Vietnamese, Indian, Japanese, and Hunan restaurants, too.

For Italian food, day in and day out you can't beat Vanessi's, although Modesto Lanzone's is awfully good, as is La Pergola. Unfortunately, the image of Italian food has been distorted through the influence of many heavy-handed restaurants that persist in serving murdered pasta with nasty, heavy, simmered-to-death tomato sauce. If Grandma simmered her special spaghetti sauce all day, it was because she was an uninformed geek who had watched one too many Ragu commercials on the tube.

Italian cuisine is among the most diverse and brilliant in the world, but it is totally dependent upon fresh ingredients, spontaneous preparation, and cooks who are imaginative, vigorous, and possess a generous and compassionate spirit. Italian dishes, like Mexican dishes, are seldom done well outside the regions of their origin.

For seafood, one is well advised to steer clear of the tourist ninnyism of Fisherman's Wharf, and stick to someplace like Tadich's or Scott's on Lombard. Or else order dishes made with fresh crab or salmon or whatever at good French, Italian, Chinese or continental places like Jack's or Ernie's.

My favorite French restaurant in the city is Le Castel out on Sacramento Street. It is arguably the best restaurant in San Francisco, except that it seems pointless to make that kind of statement because there are so many other wonderful places. When Sam Lawrence, the publisher, was in town, I took him over there knowing he'd love it. Sam devotes the same attention to getting good food and wine as another man might to freeing his foreskin from a hastily raised zipper. You need a wallet full of credit cards to eat there—you probably wouldn't want to carry that much cash around the streets—but it's well worth it. I got lucky on this particular night; Sam outgrappled me.

I think we had a lobster bisque and an exquisite appetizer of quail *en croûte*. The entrées were boned squab with chanterelles and green peppercorns in a honey-vinegar sauce, and an almost surreal pressed duck with pink peppercorns that was so beautifully presented I could barely stand to touch it with my fumbling knife and fork. We naturally availed ourselves of the very pleasant wine list.

My discovery of Le Castel was a black day for my otherwise long-suffering banker, who has since checked into an intensive care ward with high blood pressure and terminal ulcers. He wanted to know why I couldn't do something I could afford, like jump into an ice-cold river and float downstream for four or five miles.

I can't help myself. Think of it: salmon mousse awash in a *beurre blanc* in which sea urchins were puréed, then sautéed and garnished with a crayfish, or breast of pheasant in black-currant sauce, or saddle of lamb with fresh tarragon served with veal- and lamb-kidney mousse, or scallop and salmon pâté with lobster sauce, or rouget or lotte or barbue—all magnificently prepared—and a perfectly stunning array of desserts, all served by a battalion of well-informed, charming and energetic waiters.

Our arrival back at the dock is always unheralded. The dockmaster and other nautical types who never seem to do anything but watch the boats come and go never see us unload any fish although we go out every day. One of them asked about this once, and our answer—that we didn't like to see the tarpon get too tired—seemed to alert the good old boys that there was something half a bubble off-level about the three fatsos. Now they sort of look the other way when we tie up.

Even though we are now tired, sunburned, hot and irritable, we must make some stops on the way home. First is the Overseas Market, a vegetable store where we've been shopping for years. They have gingerroot and shallots, leeks, pea pods, new potatoes, avocados, good fruit, and all the other assorted vegetables we ever need to prepare the overly large, overly elaborate, overly rich meals with which we daily shorten our lives.

The next stop is essential if we expect to remain alcoholics: Big Daddy's Liquors. There we are sure to stock up on Stolichnaya, Barbancourt or Mount Gay rum, scotch and whatever wine we can find, though getting anything very good is always a problem in Key West.

We then go to Faustos, where, among other things, Harrison insists we buy the ingredients for a *puttanesca* sauce—mainly tomatoes, garlic, olives and anchovies—"In case we get hungry at four in the morning just before turning in."

Last stop is the fish market on Duval near the adult bookstore, a most inappropriately named establishment.

"The yellowtail looks good, and the guy says it's fresh."

"Okay. And I'm getting some stone-crab claws no matter what you think."

"Let's go look at the dildos and stuff."

"My God, look at the size of the double-ender!"

"Yeah, well look at this magazine, *Ass Master's Special*. Or here's *Girls Who Like Big Cocks*."

"Put that down. There's no point in you looking at that."

"Let's buy a couple of poppers and then go over to the Havana Docks and watch the hippies clap when the sun sets."

I never would have guessed that shooting was the national sport of France until I went there. From about September through the end of the year, every single man, woman and child in the entire country discharges a firearm at least once at something that walks or flies. In conversation about it, your French upland bird hunter is extremely intense and colorfully descriptive. He uses the term *paff* to indicate his gunshot, and the term *plaff* to indicate the sound of his bird hitting the ground. *Paff! Paff! Plaff!* Like that.

A couple of seasons ago I was there with Guy, Michel Jeuffrain, Jimmy Buffett and Bob Dattila, ostensibly to hunt pheasants, pigeons, partridges and ducks. We shot the pigeons from high towers constructed in the woods, the pheasant and partridge were driven to us by beaters, and the ducks were somehow just there.

At the beginning of our visit, we stayed at a huge, marvelous, renovated mill, which rivaled the magnificent 14th-century château on the same property. The house was so large we found ourselves consistently unable to locate either each other's rooms or our own. We constantly opened wrong doors only to discover yet another huge room hung with paintings, with yet another old couple seated in front of yet another Sony color television set.

Anyway, the duck hunt was something of an afterthought, because our host felt the pigeons appeared that morning in insufficient numbers. We were directed to station ourselves around the château. This seemed deeply odd, so I asked Michel where in the hell they thought the ducks were going to come from.

"Do not worry monsieur, they will arrive."

And arrive they did, about ten minutes after our host had rousted them off his lake. Wings set, the fifty or so mallards came dropping back in to home base. Only thirty-eight of them made it.

Guy and I fixed the birds that evening and it was a wonderful treat for me to cook in this provincial kitchen with its large pantry filled with fresh herbs and garden vegetables. We ate all the ducks with a great French Bordeaux, and ended up covered with grease, drunk, and totally silly.

One might convincingly argue that Parisians live for food, love and fashion, not necessarily in that order. In the morning, over croissants and coffee with their lovers, they discuss lunch, and at lunch they argue about dinner, and at dinner they are thinking of bed. They dress appropriately for all four.

The eating seemed endless to us, a dirty job as it were. But someone had to do it. We had tiny red and gray shrimp and five kinds of oysters at La Coupole one day, a classic veal roast at Lipp the next, and an elegant little meal at Castel's the day after that.

One night we ate at Kaspia, the caviar dealers, in a kind of upstairs Russian Tea Room. We opened a kilo of the finest gray caviar in the world, fresh from the Caspian Sea, the tiny, perfect eggs languishing sensually in their unique container. We had a superb vodka, commercially unavailable outside of Russia, which our host provided. After the caviar was gone, we had Scottish smoked salmon with blintzes, and to finish, a beautifully clear borscht. You couldn't have a simpler or more regal meal.

Perhaps the single most extraordinary meal we had was at the restaurant Faugeron. When entered it was very quiet, all the other customers were sheiks, and there were more waiters than patrons, all clues as to what these little snacks were going to set us back.

They didn't have the ragoût of truffles that night, a dish Guy had assured me was one of the most remarkable on the face of the earth. They did, however, have the saddle of hare, which, beyond any shadow of a doubt, is the single most delightful bit of food I've ever tasted.

When we departed Paris, I had gained about twenty pounds, my face was continually flushed and simply breathing was difficult. One afternoon at the Louvre I nearly passed out after eating a gargantuan lunch with Buffett and Dattila somewhere along the Seine. I thought for sure it was the big moment, but it wasn't.

The Havana Docks bar is a very nice place to have some drinks. We go there just about every evening at around sundown to have a few. Tonight we've had about six and they were very large, so, predictably enough, we are now drunk. Following in the great tradition of the people of every civilization since the beginning of recorded history, we are absolutely shitfaced.

"Jim," I say, "about a month ago in San Francisco I was listening to the radio and on the news they said the highway patrol reported that an unidentified man had fallen out of his car on the Golden Gate Bridge. They said it happened about six o'clock in the morning when he was on the way home from a birthday party and he stood up through the open sun roof to take off his shirt. You know why he fell out of his car? I'll tell you why. It was because that fellow had had too much to drink."

"Ungh." Harrison's eye stares off to one side at a potted palm. "What are you telling me? That we should never go to birthday parties or wear shirts?"

"I don't know, but I'm just very fond of picturing that driverless car gradually coming to a stop about three hundred yards away from its former operator. I also think we should shitcan our original plans for dinner and just walk across the street to Chez Emile, go up and sit on the balcony and order ourselves some bottles of Montrachet and a roast duck."

Swiveling efficiently off his bar stool, Guy says softly, "You got it."

In Honolulu, a tourist guide called "This Week in Oahu" advertises a restaurant called Bagwell's. A photograph of the handsome sommelier is accompanied by the slogan, "The Bagwell's Evening . . . more than an evening, it is an event." Someone told me that dinner for three there had run them around eight hundred dollars. For reasons not known to God or my mom, this did not seem to deter me. It was, in fact, more like waving a red flag in front of a bull. One can drink drinks that look like lawn furniture, and eat barbequed ribs or pizzas that taste like old socks and used Kleenex respectively for only so long. Bagwell's it was, then.

Before going to Bagwell's I was quite peckish, so it seemed sensible to eat a couple of sweet Chinese sausages, washed down with two vodka tonics. After that, I walked over to the Hyatt Regency where I was to meet my date. There we had two gigantic Bombay gin martinis at a bar called Trappers. At the restaurant itself we started with oysters (very small and fresh), shrimp bisque (tasty), terrine of veal sweetbreads (excellent), pork and veal pâté (okay), papaya, avocado, shrimp and watercress vinaigrette (perfect), and a bottle of Montrachet (just right!). After that it was *tournedos Rossini* (only about a C-plus), veal chop with truffles (much better), potatoes au gratin and French green beans (ho hum), and a bottle of Heitz Martha's

Vineyard Cabernet (yes!). To finish, there were several snifters of a very good Napoleon cognac (what could be finer?), and I skated out of there for just a shade above two-fifty, completely dizzy, stuffed, and six pounds heavier.

The night being young, illegal drugs came immediately to mind, but none could be located. Instead, I cleverly chopped up half a dozen diet pills and snorted the whole mess. Then it was off to a very interesting nightclub where, with plenty of cocktails, we watched beautiful women perform feats of imagination and daring with their private parts. For instance, one girl stacked quarters on top of a beer bottle, then had intercourse with the pile of quarters and the beer bottle, removed the bottle, and then proceeded to hand out quarters to patrons in any denomination she wished. Another girl played a pretty good flute using her you know what. She also wrote little cards to people while she was sitting on a swing holding the pen in the same place. My handwriting isn't nearly that good. After that she swung with abandon out toward the audience, a bright-green fluorescent dildo held firmly between her legs until, at the height of her forward trajectory, she fired it end over end across the club. The first one hit a bewildered Samoan in the chest. I caught mine and took it home.

The last act was performed by a vivacious and beautiful lady named Kim. She first appeared onstage in an outrageous feathered costume, which she soon removed. At the end of her dance, she squeezed out a hardboiled egg which rolled onto the stage. She then peeled it, rinsed it with Heinekens and put it back. Thus loaded, she fired this and subsequent eggs great distances and with uncanny accuracy. Later, she instructed me to open my mouth, which I did, and she whipped out a line drive that scored a bull's eye.

I liked the acts so well I insisted we stay for the second show (which gave us a chance to have a few more cocktails). For some unknown reason, I began compulsively eating the popcorn which was on our table. Three boxes of popcorn and about ten straight vodkas later the show was over and it was time to go.

Did we go home? No. Instead we decided to play some Space Invaders—right after having a few more smashed up diet pills which would be sure to sharpen the old eye. If you don't know what Space Invaders is, I'm not going to tell you. It's just the most important thing in Hawaii, that's all.

Across from the Space Invader game room was a cowboy bar where you could repair for a little refreshment, something I did frequently since my firing rocket always got blown up right away. At the time, there was the distinct feeling we hadn't yet had enough to drink.

About four in the morning I had a beer, some salami and Japanese crackers, two Alka Seltzers (in the beer), a tranquilizer, a codeine tablet and a Bufferin. Before passing out I recall being pleased to have survived the Bagwell's Evening, although I'm sure this is not precisely what the tourist guides had in mind.

It has gotten late. After finishing dinner at about midnight, we felt the need for a nightcap at the Full Moon Saloon, and of course it took a couple of hours to get that done. Now we are standing around the kitchen of our house drinking a beer at three-thirty, wondering if we should make ourselves a little pasta. In a rare display of intelligence, Guy goes to bed. Jim and I open the refrigerator and stare into it dumbly as if waiting for a recorded message to tell us what to do next.

With a certain air of resignation we close the door knowing that 1) we're too drunk to make it right, and 2) we're too tired to eat it if we did.

In my room, the house very quiet now, I find myself extremely pleased that I didn't drive to the Boca Chica bar to shoot pool until seven in the morning. As Harrison said in a poem he once gave me, what keeps you alive as an artist is chance, mobility, and sleeplessness. He's right of course, but I think I've done my job for the day, and the low-rent hustlers at the bar will have to find another boob to trick money out of this morning. My room has gotten very dark.

WILLIAM HJORTSBERG

William "Gatz" Hjortsberg (1941–2017), born in New York City, was an acclaimed author of novels and screenplays and an infinitely entertaining and intelligent man. Thomas McGuane called his first novel, *Alp* (1969), "quite possibly the finest comic novel written in America." His next three novels were *Gray Matters*, *Symbiography*, and *Toro! Toro! Toro!*; his best-known works are *Falling Angel* (filmed by Alan Parker as *Angel Heart*, with Robert De Niro and Mickey Rourke) and *Nevermore*, with Harry Houdini and Sir Arthur Conan Doyle as characters. He was also the author of *Jubilee Hitchhiker*, a biography of his close friend and neighbor Richard Brautigan.

The Fly Shop

from *Silent Seasons: Twenty-One Fishing Stories*, 1988
by William Hjortsberg

IT IS A TRIED AND TRUE angling axiom that as a fisherman grows more specialized and refined in his pursuits, the equipment he needs becomes increasingly complex and varied. Hence, the proverbial barefoot boy content to catch anything that nibbles will make do with a can of worms and a bent safety pin, while a fly fisherman after trout totes dozens of fly patterns, lines and leaders of differing weights and diameters, as well as a variety of rods, reels, waders, vests, dressings and any number of obscure doodads whose uses can only be guessed at.

This obsession with equipment was dramatically illustrated one evening several years back when a friend suggested that all attending members of Trout Unlimited bring their fishing vests along to the monthly chapter meeting. The unannounced reason for this was a prize to be awarded to the man with the most items in his vest. I don't remember who won, but the profusion of gadgets and thingamajigs was unforgettable. My own vest was a cornucopia yielding, among other things, a surgeon's hemostat (for disgorging deeply swallowed hooks), a Pink Pearl eraser (for straightening coiled leaders), a small brass-weighted club from Hardy Bros. (known in Ireland as a "priest," its use is obvious) and a spongy sheet of amadou, a highly absorbent substance prepared from fungi (for drying the hackles of waterlogged dry flies).

It is not surprising, then, considering this lifelong love affair with equipment, that a fisherman will spend almost as much time in tackle shops as he will upon a trout stream. And if a shop is not convenient, catalogs serve as reliable armchair replacements. Now that Abercrombie has become extinct, perhaps the most renowned purveyor of fishing tackle in the country is Dan Bailey in Livingston, Montana.

Over the years, Dan Bailey's Fly Shop has become something of an American institution. As the shop produces over 750,000 fishing flies annually, chances are good that the royal coachman you are securing with an improved clinch knot to your 4X leader tippet first saw the light of day at the hands of a flytier in Bailey's. For an institution, the appearance of the place is fairly low-key. Located in a one-story green stucco building on West Park Street between Gil's Got It (a gift store) and Lentfer's Taxidermy, Bailey's has less conscious decor than the average New York City dry-cleaning establishment.

The predominant interior feature, aside from the knotty-pine paneling and numbers of mounted fish, mule deer and the world's record Stone sheep, is the Wall of Fame, a collection of several hundred wooden plaques, each embellished with the silhouette of a trout four pounds or over taken on a fly. Also inscribed are the names of the lucky angler and the fly used, together with the fish's exact weight and the location of the water where the catch was made.

Among the illustrious names honored on Dan Bailey's walls are cartoonist V. T. Hamlin, creator of *Alley Oop* (4 lbs. 5 oz., badger yellow, Yellowstone R.), novelist Tom McGuane (5 lbs., spuddler, Yellowstone R.) and outdoor writers Joe Brooks (5 lbs. 5½ oz., muddler minnow, Yellowstone R.), Charlie Waterman (8 lbs. 10 oz., silver Dr., Missouri R.) and Art Flick (5 lbs. 4 oz., multicolored marabou, Yellowstone R.).

The idea for the Wall of Fame had its origins back in the middle thirties, when Dan Bailey and John McDonald shared a cabin in the Catskills and traced the outlines of their larger catches on the faded wallpaper. This practice was transplanted to the West when Bailey opened his first shop in Livingston in 1938. In those days, the store was located farther up Park Street in the old Albemarle Hotel, a fanciful, turreted brick Victorian building since replaced by a squat cinderblock motel, an example of civic vandalism which the chamber of commerce prefers to think of as "progress."

The first fish on the wall was caught on August 5, 1938, by Gilbert Meloche. He was fishing the now-famed Armstrong's Spring Creek south of town and spotted a big trout rising to a pale, near-white fly. Not having an artificial to match it, Meloche captured the insect in his hat and hurried back to Livingston, where Dan Bailey went to work at his tying bench and came up with a cream-colored fly that is known to this day as the Meloche. Back to Armstrong's, clutching the new creation, raced the eager angler, and half an hour later he returned to the Fly Shop carrying a four-and-a-half-pound brown. The silhouette was painted directly on the wall over the tying benches and an angling tradition was born.

Dan Bailey began his career as a physics professor at Brooklyn Polytech. Preferring the trout stream to the classroom, he endeavored to find a way to make a living doing what he liked best. Initial attempts involved tying oversized dry flies for use on ladies' hats sold at Bergdorf Goodman and operating a fly-tying school in the back room of Lee Chumley's restaurant on Bedford Street in Greenwich Village. The Depression was not the most encouraging time for new endeavors, and Bailey soon went west.

Livingston was picked off a map because of its proximity to some of America's finest trout-fishing water. The Yellowstone flows through town; the Madison, the Gallatin and the Boulder are all nearby. At first, times were hard in the old quarters at the Albemarle, especially during the winter months when fishing was slow. Casting about for ways to earn money during the winter, Bailey bought a traveling shooting gallery from an itinerant concessionaire passing through town. At first this was a huge success, with local marksmen dropping in at all hours to bang away in the Fly Shop. Eventually, the novelty wore thin and the shooting gallery was sold to another traveler and disappeared down the back streets of time. The Baileys' next extracurricular enterprise was a whitefish business. Thirty-five years ago, the Rocky Mountain whitefish was not yet classified as a game species and could be sold commercially. Local fishermen brought their catches to the Fly Shop, which soon became a distribution center for area restaurants. The whitefish were cleaned, packed in ice and sold by the case.

The business thrived until one Christmas when the Baileys departed for a short vacation, leaving a friend in charge of operating the Fly Shop. Returning to Livingston weeks later, they were greeted by the overwhelming stench of rotting fish when they unlocked the front door. Their friend, it turned out, had been jailed for nonsupport and thousands of whitefish were left to decompose in the shop. The Baileys decided forthwith to get out of the whitefish business and move to an apartment in town.

But the days of shooting galleries and whitefish concessions are long gone. Today, Dan Bailey's employs between forty and fifty professional flytiers, each of whom is capable of producing six to ten dozen flies every day, depending upon the complexity of the pattern. The shop normally stocks three or four hundred different patterns, and boxes of exotic feathers, fur and yarn line the hallway in the tying section.

In addition to the standard traditional patterns, Bailey's will tie flies on special order to accommodate a customer's particular needs. The sample case, a tall wooden cabinet such as a lepidopterist might use to display his butterfly collection, holds thousands of these specialized patterns, each numbered and cataloged for easy reference. The case is a treasure trove of the bizarre and the extraordinary, an explosion of colors and textures that would make the palette of an abstract expressionist seem drab by comparison.

Although many of the special orders are useful and beautiful flies, not a few border on the ludicrous. Looking through the case, one comes across such oddities as a green sponge-rubber spider, a creature made of carpet yarn, and a fat white caterpillar that most closely resembles an unwrapped Tampax.

Perhaps the oddest special order ever tied by the shop was for a local rancher who raised trout in a spring-fed pond. These trout, like all hatchery fish, were fed on pellets and grew to enormous size. The rancher, an avid fly fisherman, watched with increasing frustration the pellet-gorged brutes cruising in the depths of his pond. No matter what fly he offered them (and he tried every pattern from an Adams to a white Miller), the trout refused to rise. In desperation, he asked Dan Bailey's to tie some flies that looked like pellets. Although displeased by the aesthetics of the assignment, the flytiers soon came up with a clipped-deer-hair creation that did the trick. Every year since then, Bailey's receives dozens of orders for "pellet flies" from fishpond owners all over the country.

Of course, fishing flies are not all that Dan Bailey's sells. The shop also carries rods, reels, creels, nets, waders, hip boots, lines, leaders, vests and tackle boxes. Everything, in fact, that a fisherman could possibly need and quite a few items he might easily do without. A micrometer for measuring leader diameters and a mosquito head net are among the more superfluous articles in stock. Twenty-five thousand catalogs listing most of this incredible inventory are mailed each year.

With all this, there is still room for a surprise discovery. I was in the shop not too long ago when a customer came in and spoke to John Bailey. Bailey nodded and went in back under the arch upon which hangs the largest trout ever taken from the Yellowstone on a fly, an unbelievable fourteen-pound four-ounce brown. As I watched, he opened a small refrigerator and matter-of-factly removed a covered cardboard container. It might have held coleslaw, but it didn't. I was speechless with the enormity of this revelation. Dan Bailey's Fly Shop also sells night crawlers!

STEPHEN BODIO

Stephen Bodio's (1950–) books include *A Rage for Falcons*, *Tiger Country*, *Eagle Dreams*, and *Aloft*, as well as several other beautifully written works. *Querencia*, which describes Bodio's love affair with Betsy Huntington and Magdalena, New Mexico, was described in *The Washington Post* as "a fine memoir, a touch sentimental but only in the right places, expert in its descriptions of nature." Annie Proulx, in her introduction to *An Eternity of Eagles*, writes, "Bodio . . . was a man who collected insects, raised pigeons, hunted with falcons and hawks; collected rare books on the natural world; was vastly well read on history, paleontology, archaeology, and climatology; knew about ancient horses, the history and habits of the dog, and ancient Egyptian mummification processes."

The Los Angeles Times described *Querencia* as "an understated elegy to a highly unconventional but fascinating woman, and to the life they shared." Stephen Bodio still lives in Magdalena, and despite suffering from Parkinson's, he maintains a blog with the help of his wife, Libby Frishman-Bodio.

from Querencia

by Stephen Bodio, 1991

IN THE HIGH COUNTRY, weather is vertical, hourly temperatures cut by the razor edge of shadows. Weather makes vegetation and vice versa; exposure shapes climate. Simple questions like "is it hotter in New Mexico?" (than in Boston, New York, or San Francisco) have no simple answers. Consider: in the summer, Magdalena's temperatures rarely break ninety degrees Fahrenheit. In the winter, forty-degree days are common, and warm thaws of nearly seventy not rare. A mild climate, you say? Not really. More than season, "climate"—we really have no exact word—can be a result of hours, vertical feet, level miles, or mere inches from sun to shade.

Those forty-degree winter days have nights that plunge into the single digits. Altitude, when all altitude is high and the air is dry, can mean differentials as harsh as those from Mexico to Canada. Socorro is in the valley and relatively humid along the river, and its summer temperatures usually top one hundred degrees. Climb ten miles to the top of the plateau and you lose ten degrees of temperature, all of the humidity, and gain a breeze. Go from there to the top of the Magdalenas four miles away and it's cool, probably in the seventies; at night, chilly. On top of the mountains frost is always a possibility.

Travel from a sunny winter day of almost fifty in Socorro onto the plateau and into its deep heart around Mangas. The total rise in elevation will be less than three thousand feet. But if it is a good, clear, still day—the kind that warms up the valley best—radiational cooling will make all the heat roar off into the star-studded void as soon as the sun goes down. By morning the temperature may have fallen to well below zero in Mangas.

As for dampness: if you go up into a slightly larger mountain range than the Magdalenas—say the San Mateos, twenty miles southwest and about twice as wide—you go up not only into cool but also toward meadows lush as an English park, often complete with grazing stags. You'll find fields of blue flag irises, little *ciénagas* or marshes, springs, and above that a Canadian profusion of fir and spruce. Big, high mountains hold the weather and wring the clouds.

The whole concept of "life zones," a vertical array of landscapes from Sonoran up through Canadian to Hudsonian (as in Hudson Bay), taught to us in bygone freshman biology courses, was born in C. Hart Merriam's brain as he looked at western mountains. It's still a useful metaphor, though as usual reality tends to be a bit more complicated. Sure, there are broad bands of like vegetation, as visible as rock strata in a stream cut. After October a straight horizontal line, white above, blue-brown below, forms on the Magdalenas. Above it, roughly at the line between the piñon-juniper and the higher, more conventionally pine-like ponderosa, the snow stays until May, forming drifts three feet deep in the sunless ravines of the northern slopes. Below it we get a snowstorm every couple of weeks, at least at Magdalena's six thousand-plus feet. But—another difference between the dry west and the flatlands—the snow vanishes until the next storm.

I didn't say "melts," though some of it certainly does. A lot of it just sublimes away, sucked back into the air by a ferocious combination of sun and dry wind. But the difference between sun and shade temperatures in high, clear places is unlike anything at sea level. At the north side of the house, where the cold, blue shade lasts all winter while the sun withdraws to the south, there is always one little patch of snow, huddled as if for safety between the adobe wall and the propane tank. It lasts for months, though the rest of the yard is brown sand and dry, brown grass. And when you stand beside it in that shade, you feel winter's chill even when, on the other side of the house, you could warm your back on sun-heated stucco and bask in fifty degrees of winter warmth. The same goes for summer. Ninety dry, skin-crisping degrees in the sun can turn into cool and comfortable beneath the Siberian elms. Is New Mexico hotter or cooler than New England?

All this jigsaw puzzle of sun and shade and altitude determines the flora. What grows where may not sound very important to those who live in well-watered climates, where everything left alone becomes first a green fuzz of weeds, then a tangled thicket, finally a forest. But here "sky determines," as New Mexican historian Ross Calvin said. Besides the life zones, vegetation differs from northern to southern exposures. Canyon sides facing south have lower altitude, more Mexican, more arid-type growth: oaks, yuccas, few large conifers. Northern-facing exposures, where the sun doesn't shine in the winter, are more Canadian; the snow builds deep and stays long, under tall poles of ponderosa pine. This pattern gives an oddly comforting sense of direction, like a biological compass.

Animal habitat is vertical too. Clark's nutcrackers, large noisy birds like pallid crows with bold black-and-white wing flags, appear only on the highest peaks, geese and cranes only on the Rio Grande. Between are hardy species that roam everywhere like coyotes and ravens, and rarer ones that live only in specific island habitats. Red-faced warblers, tiny ground-creeping songbirds in drab gray with brilliant red-and-black hoods, live only in a narrow band of oak thickets in south-facing canyons, at about sixty-five hundred feet. Some animals even make vertical migrations. In the winter goshawks, Cooper's hawks and sharp-shins descend from the piney forests where they breed to fall on the town like avian wolves. They skulk in cottonwoods and twist and turn between the walls of Magdalena's houses exactly as they do between the tree trunks of their summer home, chasing sparrows and starlings that in turn live off the leavings of pigs and goats and fighting chickens. Nobody bothers them much, and so they are sometimes startling in their boldness; they'll stop and sit on a tree in the yard and turn to check you out, or kill a sparrow in the snow outside the window and stare up with their terrible orange-yellow cartoon eyes, as though weighing the odds of taking you down. So, in other times, must wolves have descended on winter villages.

Brightness, New Mexico's enchanted light, is the stuff of tourist brochures and coffee-table books: spotlit mountains, ruddy afterglow, white peaks above blue ranges, above warm plains the color of a mountain lion's pelt. It's almost a cliché. But it is this thin, bright air that makes it possible to see so far so clearly and therefore paradoxically think that things are smaller and closer together, like things back home in Kansas or Massachusetts. The foothills surrounding Magdalena are sprinkled with juniper. These range from eight to twenty feet high and are spaced at roughly equal distances, never clumped. When you look up from the plain you see them as separate dark heads, scattered like grains of pepper. Your eastern eyes will tell you they are bushes, knee- or waist-high, and pretty close, not trees four or five miles away.

We'd always ask visitors how far back from the road they thought Ladron's bare peak was. Westerners had little trouble. Easterners would look and say "a mile" or, if adventurous, "three or four miles." Try again. From the nearest point on Route 60 to the tip of Ladron is twenty-seven miles. We'd try to convince them.

"See that ribbon at the foot? Use the binoculars."

"Yeah, so what?"

"That's the bluffs along the Rio Grande. Look on the map. That's twenty miles in."

"I don't believe it."

If it were summer we'd never convince them, at least not down in that core where people really believe. But in winter . . .

"Okay. See those blue ridges beyond the peak, to the right a little? Two big curves? Right, there. Do they remind you of anything?"

Most wouldn't get it at first. But eventually the white upper edges, the parallel bands of subtle tints, begin to tug at memory. "They look a little like the mountains over Albuquerque. And the ones south of there when we drove down the river."

"That's what they are. The Sandias—ninety miles away. And the Manzanos, a little south."

Nothing gets in the way.

The light can be dangerous. Not in the clichéd way of old westerns, burning down to fry you in the desert like an egg on a sidewalk. Though I suppose it's possible to suffer such a fate in New Mexico, it's more likely in the low, hot and utterly arid Sonoran Desert to the west. Rather, the light will get you in more subtle ways, if anything about New Mexico's blazing sunlight is subtle. Up this high you are less shielded from ultraviolet rays, from cosmic radiation, than down in more normal, humane habitats. You squint and get headaches and wear sunglasses and squeeze deep lines into the tissue around your eyes. Skin turns leathery early. And if you expose and burn it too much, especially if you are an Anglo, it will finally spot and turn strange and grow cancers. New Mexico has the highest rate in the nation of two odd ways to die—bubonic plague and skin cancer. It's not a place for sunbathers. Even a swarthy half-Italian like me feels a deep physical prickling and unease if I stay exposed to the sun too long, and I don't generally burn. We all may have red (or brown) necks, but we all also wear long pants and long-sleeved western shirts and, above all, broad-brimmed hats. Out here, "cowboy" clothes are a necessity, not a fad.

RICK BASS

Rick Bass (1958–), now also renowned as an environmental activist, was raised in Texas and was working as a petroleum geologist in Jackson, Mississippi, when he began writing the stories that eventually became *The Watch* (1989). When he and his wife Elizabeth Hughes first moved to Montana, they visited us at Deep Creek, and when Rick wrote about the Ninemile pack for *Outside*, and wanted to expand the story into a book, he felt Clark City was the right place. There was some dueling with Sam Lawrence of Houghton Mifflin, and half the edits arrived on postcards sent from the road, but being able to publish an account of the rewilding of the state was probably the greatest honor of my time at Clark City. Since then Rick has written more than thirty books of nonfiction and short stories, including the recent collection *With Every Great Breath* (Counterpoint). His work has appeared in *The Atlantic*, *The New Yorker*, and *The Paris Review*. In *The New York Times*, Dwight Garner wrote that Bass's stories "display clarity and heart and moral vision, and glow like a well-tended wood stove." Rick brings this same passion to his nonfiction and his activism on behalf of the natural world. He's received Guggenheim and NEA fellowships, as well as the Pushcart Prize, the Story Prize, and the O. Henry Award. He still lives in the Yaak Valley of Montana.

from

The Ninemile Wolves

by Rick Bass, 1992

WHERE THE STORY STARTED for our species—where humans picked up on the scent and fell into the chase—was in Pleasant Valley, a long, narrow valley in northwestern Montana lying roughly midway between Glacier National Park and the town of Libby. Northwestern Montana's not great cattle country—it's too cold, too snowy, and there's not much grass (mostly timber, or steep rocks, or ragged moonscape clear-cuts)—but near the tiny village of Marion, in April of 1989, a two-year-old male wolf (probably not a Glacier wolf) tried to get in a sheep pen one night. The line of intersection between wolf and man in Montana had been crossed after roughly sixty years of silence,[5] and from this point there wouldn't be, and probably won't be, any turning back: no more silence.

Certain wolves will prey on cattle, and to a greater extent, upon hapless, irresistible sheep; anyone who tells you a wolf won't kill a cow or sheep is lying or misinformed. But there is an almost infinite number of variables. Wild, healthy wolves tend to stay away from livestock. A wolf that has never been "taught" by its elders to hunt or eat livestock probably never will.

One of the trouble times for wolves as well as coyotes with regard to livestock depredation is in April, when the pups have just been born and the whole pack is hanging around the den for a few months, still unable to travel. Deer and elk in the area tend to get understandably spooked by a three-month wolf pack *encampment*. The wolves' nutritional demands are greater then, with extra hunting required to take care of the pups and, I propose (which I can do, being a writer and not a biologist), it's possible that the rest of the pack gets plain restless during the denning period. Typically

5 There was one brief and fatal (for cows) flurry of cow-wolf interaction on the Blackfeet Reservation, east of the Continental Divide, in 1987.

(though not always) only the alpha male and female will have bred, and from April to July of each year the rest of the pack just stays near the den, waiting. The cattle call may beckon to restless wolves in the spring.

In July, the pack starts to move the pups a little farther from the den to "rendezvous" sites—usually places where some animal has been killed—and the pups begin to learn what the game's about by eating these on-site kills, and by chasing mice and grasshoppers. By late August or September, the pups, which grow quickly, are ready to start traveling, ready to start watching "real" hunts.

The wolf that had been—or rather, had allegedly been—trying to get in the Marion area sheep pen was shot and killed by the rancher; the rancher said he thought it was a dog or coyote, but when he realized it could be a wolf, he called authorities. The incident was investigated by USF&WS agents, and the rancher wasn't prosecuted. It turned out ranchers and other residents had been hearing wolves for some time prior to the shooting, but hadn't reported them for the usual reason: fear that all kinds of federal restraints might be placed upon the valley. Some kind of quarantine, perhaps, is how I picture the ranchers imagining it—a giant plastic bubble being placed over the valley, with a blood mist being sprayed by helicopter every six hours to further incite the wolves, and ranchers being handcuffed to their beds each night as they listen to the bleats and bawls of their sheep and cattle . . .

The reality is that wolves preying on livestock on private lands are "removed" immediately, and there is little doubt that this is anything but beneficial to both wolf and rancher, though there are numerous cases where wolves have stopped killing cattle after two or three depredations. The line has been crossed—humans have contacted wolves again, and wolves have contacted humans—and it's important for the wolves and the humans that we try to avoid the bitter polarization that characterizes other environmental battles. Readers should note at this point in the story that there hadn't been any livestock depredation—just howling—although a wolf (maybe the two-year-old male, but maybe another, older male) had been seen among livestock on several occasions. Because there's a $100,000 fine and a one-year jail term for killing a wolf, ranchers were concerned, seeing this wolf frolic with their livestock, but were hesitant to try to remove it themselves.

In late July, four months after the two-year-old was killed in a sheep pen, a wolf rendezvous site (and possible den) was discovered only three miles from the sheep corral. USF&WS personnel asked the rancher to let them leave the wolves on his ranch until late August—to let the pups mature. Wolf packs are wired so intricately, with such complexity, that there's not a single record of a pack being busted up by humans and then reassembling itself. The rancher agreed to let the pups stay on his land through the month. He frequently observed the wolves hunting small mammals among his cattle.

After August the pack's integrity would be destroyed if trapped and relocated, but the individuals should survive. Things were just too tense: too many cattle, too many sheep, too close to the wolves. The USF&WS had data from Minnesota that showed pups had high survival chances after August even if separated from their pack, and if the pups weighed over thirty-five pounds. These numbers, while ultimately not safe enough for the pups in the Marion case, may prove important to the rest of wolf history in the United States, and should be remembered, and perhaps increased slightly.

On August 21st, 1989, fortune's winds shifted. A domestic dog was attacked (allegedly) by two wolves—a large gray wolf and a smaller black one. Wild wolves *hate* dogs in their territory, viewing them as competitors, and kill and eat them with gusto. On that same day a rancher found five dead calves and one severely wounded calf.

On the 22nd of August, a USF&WS biologist, an Animal Damage Control[6] specialist and a Montana Department of Fish, Wildlife & Parks (MDFWP) conservation officer checked out the remains. The battles had occurred in a pasture that had been holding exclusively sick and weakened calves. The data gathered by the federal officials and a veterinarian, wrote Ed Bangs, a federal wolf biologist down from Alaska, "suggested wolves were not responsible for injuries to the surviving calf but that the attack came from a smaller inefficient canine predator." There were, and still are, a lot of coyotes in the Marion area, and coyotes generally kill by choking the victim, rather than pulling the prey down from behind—grabbing the flanks with their teeth—which is more typical of wolves than coyotes.

Regardless of the lack of evidence against wolves—despite, in fact,

6 A federally and state-funded predator eradication program with an annual budget of $45,000,000.

evidence which pointed to coyotes—the USF&WS decided that day to proceed with their relocation; had already decided before the incident, in fact, to go ahead with it the very next day.

"One day," Ed Bangs lamented, stroking the black handlebar moustache that gives him the look of a circus lion tamer. "Just one more day, and we would have had them out of there."

Wolf recovery in Montana was in its most embryonic stages. This was the first known pack to have a den outside of the park[7] in over sixty years, the first *expansion*, and whether it was coyotes or wolves that had killed the livestock was irrelevant: The public perception was that wolves were in there doing the killing, and such a cow-killing catastrophe the first time wolves were seen out of the park could have meant the end of the wolf recovery program before it had really begun. I want to believe the wolves were pure—that it was coyotes who deviled those sick cows, and then the young wolves and alpha female moved in and scavenged afterward—but word was out, *belief* was out, and the situation wasn't going to disappear.

It took three days before traps (leg-hold, spring-action) could be set, due to rain. There are basically only two ways to catch wolves alive—by leg-hold traps, or by tranquilizing (darting)—and northwest Montana's timbered so heavily that the helicopter chases so effective for getting close to wolves to tranquilize them are frequently impossible.

A third method of capture is sometimes available and should be mentioned, though it bears a certain repellence to the spirit: Trapped wolves may be fitted with radio collars which, in addition to transmitting the wolves' location, contain injectors which, so goes the theory, can be remote-controlled to fire tranquilizers into the wolf's neck, dropping the wolf long-distance, on command—a notion eerily similar to those high-pitched dog whistles advertised in boys' magazines, or worse yet, a leash.

The traps were set August 25th. Three wolves had been observed near the rendezvous site: a black female and two pups. Two of the pups (both female "young-of-the-year," born in April) were captured immediately. They weighed forty and forty-one pounds. It was still raining. The mother could not be caught, nor could any additional wolves. One of the greatest things

7 A den was found on the Blackfeet Reservation, east of Glacier, in 1987, which was believed to have been used that year.

about wolf packs is that you can never be entirely sure how many are in a pack. The social hierarchy of alpha male and alpha female, of baby-sitting aunts and occasionally uncles, and of outcasts living sometimes just out of sight of the pack, is always tense, ripe for change, and at least partially obscured to everyone but the wolves themselves. By the fall, even the pups, at sixty to eighty pounds, are hard to distinguish from the adults, who may weigh only seventy to one hundred pounds.

The pups were put in a veterinary clinic in Kalispell, then brought back out to the rendezvous site and placed in individual kennels in the hopes that the adult female would remain close to her pups' cages. Every three to four days thereafter, the pups were taken back into the clinic for examination. The state agency—the MDFWP—provided road-killed deer to keep the pups fed.

On August 28th, parts of a full-grown cow—hind leg, front leg, ribs, vertebrae—were found at the wolves' rendezvous site, as were fresh wolf scats containing red and black cow hair. It's possible that the coyotes did the killing and then the larger remaining wolf, or wolves, might have run the coyotes off the kill. But in the climate of panic it didn't look good for the wolves, and in Minnesota such evidence would have been classified as "confirmed wolf depredation."

Two more days passed. USF&WS stayed in close contact with local ranchers and held a meeting in which, according to Ed Bangs, "only a couple of individuals seemed very upset about the presence of wolves." The ranchers' main concern, Bangs says, was what would happen back up in the woods, where the ranchers couldn't see what was going on—the eternal, lovely metaphor of the wolf's existence: his dark shape, just beyond the edge of the dark woods.

Another cow, a 300-pound calf, was killed in the same "sick" pasture. This made six known calf depredations. Coyotes were seen running from the carcass. Wounds—hemorrhaging in the throat—suggested coyotes. Coyote tracks and scats were all around the area. Bangs wrote, "Service personnel elicited howling from two large groups of coyotes near the pasture on several nights."

The next day, the calf that was still living but severely wounded was killed by the rancher and skinned and examined. Bite wounds indicated coyotes or, possibly, very young wolves, because the skin was never entirely punctured, only scraped, as if the predator had strangled the calf. In some places teeth had broken through the hide but in other places had only scraped the skin. One set of bites measured two and one-sixteenth inches wide, implying a wolf, but the bite marks could have come from two separate snaps.

Labor Day passed. Several coyotes were trapped, but no additional wolves. The two wolf pups continued to be shuttled back and forth from vet clinic to rendezvous site, to be used as a lure.

On September 7th, a new wolf showed up in one of the USF&WS traps: an old gray male with extreme tooth wear, including his canines. His teeth were more worn than any wolf the biologists had ever seen. His front left foot was injured by the trap. His front canine teeth measured two and one-sixteenth inches across.

It was time to get on with the show, to walk away from the issue or finish it. On September 8th, an Animal Damage Control (ADC) specialist shot the black female from a helicopter with an immobilizing drug, Telazol. It was a "great shot" from the helicopter, according to Ed Bangs, and she went down in only four minutes.

While under this drug, Telazol, the wolf is open-eyed, in a phase that the drug's manufacturer, the A. H. Robins Company, calls "cataleptoid anaesthesia." Do the cataleptoid wolves' open eyes relay to the mind what's going on, as they're handled by humans? No one can say for sure. The drug's pamphlet states that "the anaesthetic state produced does not fit into the conventional classification of states of anaesthesia, but instead . . . produces a state . . . which has been termed 'dissociative' anaesthesia in that it appears to selectively interrupt association pathways to the brain . . . cranial nerve reflexes remain active."

I hope that certain "associative pathways" do remain open, such as the pathways that take fear in and out of the brain. On the one hand, the terror for such a wild animal—being handled, and unable to flee—is probably unbearable; on the other hand—or so we might anthropomorphize—it could make the animal so wild and wary that its future survival ability might be heightened to new levels.

JIM HARRISON

Jim Harrison (1937–2016) was the author of forty-one works of fiction, nonfiction, and poetry, including *Dalva*, *Legends of the Fall*, the *Brown Dog* novellas, *Returning to Earth*, and *The Shape of the Journey*. He was a member of the Academy of Arts and Letters whose work was translated into more than two dozen languages. He was also, to my knowledge, the only poet to have the phrase "hot buttered cheerleaders" in his *New York Times* obituary.

My father and mother were only twenty-two and nineteen when I was born, and the writer I knew, the one who wrote *Plain Song* and *Locations*, and was granted a Guggenheim and a National Endowment and promptly ran back to the woods to write *Wolf*, is only remembered by a few people now: his sister Mary, his brother David, Tom McGuane. What I'd really like people to know is how generous he was with young writers, and how deeply he loved his friends and family and life. And what I'd most like to say: Read his poetry. It's what he loved; it's where he put his heart and mind. But if you want to feel like you're at a bar with him, the food pieces, collected in *The Raw and the Cooked* and *A Really Big Lunch*, are a good way to begin.

Hunger, Real and Unreal

from *Just Before Dark: Collected Nonfiction*, 1991
by Jim Harrison

"DID YOU EVER NOTICE how we never allow ourselves to be actually hungry?" said Russell Chatham, a burly painter of some note. We were eating a prehunt breakfast, parked beside Oleson's buffalo paddock outside Traverse City, Michigan. All of the little boy buffalo, ignorant of gender, were chasing one another around, hell-bent on sex, their red wangers bobbing in the air. "Those guys are a tad confused," Chatham added, eyeing the corked bottle of wine, at which we both coughed, thinking that ten in the morning isn't too early for a sip of red wine with a sandwich. Way up here in the northland there's a fine Italian delicatessen, Folgarelli's, and Chatham was having a hot Italian sausage with marinara sauce and melted mozzarella, while my choice was a simple prosciutto, mortadella, Genoa salami and provolone on an Italian roll.

Throughout the day we mulled over the not-exactly-metaphysical question of why we never, for more than a moment, allowed ourselves to be hungry. Could this possibly be why we were both seriously overweight? But only a fool jumps to negative conclusions about food, especially before dinner. *Cuisine minceur* notwithstanding, the quality of food diminishes sharply in proportion to negative thinking about ingredients and, simply put, the amount to be prepared. There is no substitute for Badia a Coltibuono olive oil. Period. Or the use of salt pork in the cooking of southwest France. Three ounces of Chablis are far less interesting and beneficial than a magnum of Bordeaux. I have mentioned before that we are in the middle of yet another of the recurrent sweeps across our nation of the "less is more" bullies. When any of these people arrive in my yard, I toss a head of lettuce and some dog biscuits off the porch.

Despite these apparent truths, almost biblical in veracity, and bearing some of the grandeur of our Constitution, I recently learned that hunger is the actual sensation of the body burning its own fat. This is not a very appetizing idea but is, nonetheless, a positive experience when the body wears too much fat. I learned this when I spent two weeks at the Rancho La Puerta health spa in Tecate, Mexico, in order to quit smoking.

Almost incidentally I lost seventeen pounds. This appears impossible, but some of it was "easy" weight from a feast (the usual wonderful squid, chicken, tuna, carpaccio, lamb, etc.) at Rondo's in Los Angeles the evening before my incarceration. I also worked out six to eight hours a day: I took a solo four-hour mountain hike each morning to look for birds and follow the tracks of coyote, bobcat, and puma, and I did up to three hours of exercise in the gym.[8]

Now this was an unconscionable and pathetic amount of exertion, but necessary to avoid cigarettes. I plummeted into a depression in which the first of my ideals to fly away into the mountains was literature. The Rancho's menu was vegetarian with fish twice a week. Chef Ramon Flores took this limited cuisine as far as it can be taken, but not quite far enough for the grief of a man who had temporarily lost his calling. One late morning after an exhausting hike, I began to tremble uncontrollably, a state I recognized as protein starvation. A tumbler of Herradura tequila was a temporary measure until I gathered the strength to call a cab and head into town for a slab of swordfish with garlic sauce and a full order of *carne asada.*

Quite naturally, as Americans we all loathe decadence, though our notions of decadence change from time to time. Around the turn of the century, a man's girth was a fair estimate of his prosperity and moral worth, and the thin, sallow look, so much the rage at present, was considered fair evidence of low birth and probable criminal intent. (Curiously enough, of the countless times I've been swindled in Hollywood, the guilty parties have always been thin.) Men nowadays will not settle for a Paul Newman washboard stomach but want an entire washboard body, even though none of them remembers an actual washboard in his past.

Let's all stop a moment in our busy day and return to some eternal verities. It's quite a mystery, albeit largely unacknowledged, to be alive, and, quite

8 Never. —Editor

simply, in order to remain alive you must keep eating. My notion, scarcely original, is that if you eat badly you are very probably living badly. You tend to eat badly when you become inattentive to all but the immediate economic necessities, real or imagined, and food becomes an abstraction; you merely "fill up" in the manner that you fill a car with gasoline, no matter that some fey grease slinger has put raspberry puree on your pen-raised venison. You are still a nitwit bent over a trough.

At the Rancho one day at lunch I told some plumpish but kindly ladies what I thought was a charming story of simple food. One August, years ago, I was wandering around the spacious property of a château up in Normandy, trying to work up a proper appetite for lunch. The land doubled as a horse farm, and a vicious brood mare had tried to bite me, an act I rewarded with a stone sharply thrown against her ass. Two old men I hadn't seen laughed beneath a tree. I walked over and sat with them around a small fire. They were gardeners and it was their lunch hour, and on a flat stone they had made a small circle of hot coals. They had cored a half-dozen big red tomatoes, stuffed them with softened cloves of garlic, and added a sprig of thyme, a basil leaf, and a couple of tablespoons of soft cheese. They roasted the tomatoes until they softened and the cheese melted. I ate one with a chunk of bread and healthy-sized swigs from a jug of red wine. When we finished eating, and since this was Normandy, we had a sip or two of calvados from a flask. A simple snack but indescribably delicious.

I waited only a moment for the ladies' reaction. *Cheese*, two of them hissed, *cheese*, as if I had puked on their sprouts, and *wine*! The upshot was that cheese is loaded with cholesterol and wine has an adverse effect on blood sugar. I allowed myself to fog over as one does while reading bad reviews of one's own work.

That evening, Gael Greene, also a Rancho guest, spoke of the travails of being a food critic, making me ache for the usual foie gras and truffles. Later I told her that I used to carry a notebook and Dictaphone into restaurants, assuring myself of a good meal as a bogus food critic. I never actually said I was a critic, only that I couldn't talk about it. I reflected, too, on the idea of food snobbism: my friends in Paris are cynical about the idea of a good meal in New York, and in New York the idea of eating in Chicago is somewhat laughable, and so on through Los Angeles and San Francisco in every direction. I enjoy telling them that in recent years my best meal was at the Ali-Oli in San Juan, Puerto Rico. True.

At dawn the next morning I decided to spend the day in the mountains. I figured that Aldous Huxley, one of my boyhood heroes, who used to hang out at the Rancho, would have done the same thing. I took my binoculars, an orange, a hard-boiled egg, and a one-ounce bottle of Tabasco for the egg.

Four hours into the mountains I ate the egg and the orange. I was seated downwind from a bobcat cave, hoping for a sighting but knowing it was doubtful until just before dark. The cave had a dank, overpowering feline odor similar, I imagined, to that of the basement of a thousand-year-old Chinese whorehouse (the visionary propensities of hunger!).

Then out of the chaparral appeared a tough, ragged-looking Mexican who asked me if I had anything to eat. I said no, wishing I had saved the orange. He smiled, bowed, and continued scampering up Mt. Kuuchamaa, presumably toward the United States and the pursuit of happiness, including something to eat. He had chosen the most difficult route imaginable, and I followed his progress with the binoculars, deciding that not one of the Rancho's fitness buffs, including the instructors, could have managed the mountain at that speed.

I didn't feel the couch liberal's guilt over not having saved the orange for him, just plain old Midwestern Christian guilt. In my deranged state I thought that maybe the guy was Jesus, and I had denied him the orange! Then I lapsed into memories of things I had eaten when I was actually hungry, such as the fried trout I used to eat at streamside with bread and salt. I remembered, during my wandering-starving-artist years in the late 1950s, spending subway fare for a thirty-five-cent Italian-sausage sandwich and walking seventy blocks to work the next morning, eating free leftovers given to me by Babe and Louis at the Kettle of Fish bar, buying twenty-five-cent onion sandwiches on rye bread at McSorley's. I had wonderful meals while working as a poetic busboy at the Prince Brothers Spaghetti House in Boston; I often devoured two fried eggs at a diner after Storyville, the best jazz club ever, closed at dawn. In the San Francisco area there were two-for-a-nickel oranges, the oddly delicious macaroni salad at the Coexistence Bagel Shop for a quarter, the splurge of an enormous fifty-cent bowl of pork and noodles in Chinatown. And let's not forget the desperation of eating ten-cent cafeteria bread and catsup in Salt Lake City or the grapefruit given me by an old woman in the roadside dust near Fallon, Nevada.

When I arrived home from one of these trips, mostly brown skin and bones, my father said, "If you had stayed away longer, you wouldn't weigh nothing at all. It's plain to see it will be some time, if ever, before you know what you are doing, James." Then he fired up the grill, and we went into his enormous garden and picked all manner of fresh vegetables. He broiled some chickens with lemon, garlic, and butter. That's what I remembered on the way down the mountain.

Night Walking

from *Just Before Dark: Collected Nonfiction*, 1991
by Jim Harrison

IT IS AN ODDLY PROTESTANT NOTION that life is a form of punishment to be endured to reach a greater end. Even when this idea isn't allowed to be overwhelming, it's still hiding behind the curtains like a headless leper ready to reach out and grab you in case you're feeling a little too good.

Life is a vale of woe, they used to say, during my childhood in Michigan. The illustrated Bible was full of pictures of bleeding folks, vipers biting kids, sorrowful ladies, old guys sleeping on beds of rags, rocks and ashes. If we survived the Nazis and Japs, that wouldn't prevent God, in all his justified anger, from snuffing out the sun, moon and stars. At the end of the road was probably the Lake of Fire, but before that could be reached, there was a lot of hard work and grinding poverty to go through. My own distinct case history reached its theological nadir when I was blinded in one eye at age seven by a little girl wielding a broken bottle. We had our clothes off in a heavily wooded vacant lot on an exploratory venture.

A severe childhood injury is not a bad preparation for life in this portion of the twentieth century. It makes you empathetic and wary, and you lack the built-in compass your friends seem to have: fence posts and trees contort into question marks, and at any moment you might fall through the earth where the crust is thin. Much later, certain news photos would have a natural resonance: the girl's mouth torn open in a simian howl at Kent State, and the Vietnamese girl trotting nudely down the road after a napalm bath. Happier images are arrayed above my desk: a crow wing and a heron wing, an antisuicide button, a dried grizzly turd, a small toy pig, a Haitian baby shoe found on the beach in Florida after a boatload of refugees had been carted off to jail, having missed the Statue of Liberty by a thousand miles.

The northern Midwest night I grew up in was the only immediately available mystery, other than the bombazine Saturday matinees featuring the likes of Roy Rogers and the Sons of the Pioneers. There was a whole theater full of village and farm kids trying to figure out what tumbleweed was, only to be released back out into a black sky and immense snowbanks. Years later, while hitchhiking to California, I was in a car accident and finally saw tumbleweed an inch from my nose and heard again the warbling of the Pioneers.

But summer nights, winter nights and walking. My father, who owned the unlikely name of Winfield Sprague Harrison, built a cabin on a lake with the help of his brothers for the grand sum of a thousand dollars in 1946. My uncles had just returned from full-term service in World War II and were particularly kind to me as one of the fellow injured. I took walks with them and was referred to as Little Beaver, after the Red Ryder comic strip. Then, while my uncles busied themselves fishing or getting drunk, I began to walk during the day and evening alone. I discovered that twilight was a fine time to walk, and night herself was even more wonderful. I walked along creeks and a river and around the lake, with the voices of bass fishermen carrying to the shore. Once, through a cabin window, I saw a nude girl dancing with a Dalmatian dog in the light of an oil lamp; another time I saw a very old couple in utter hysterics listening to "Fibber McGee and Molly" on a battery-operated radio. The old man slid off his chair, kicking his feet with laughter. The old woman helped him back up on the couch, and they began pelting each other with popcorn. There was no electric power in the area, so night was truly dark.

I envied Jesus' ability to walk on water, imagining how I would look down through the surface of the lake as if it were glass, observing the secret lives of fishes and turtles and the fabled and elusive water bird, the loon, which could swim faster underwater, it was said, than the penguin or dolphin, a Jap torpedo or a German submarine.

I had a particular spot favored for a big moon—a grove of white birches where deer wandered and where, if you stupidly missed the point, you could read a newspaper in the shimmering light. Blue herons lived near the grove, and they often fished in the shallows on bright nights. There was a Chippewa Indian burial mound, and a girl I knew said if you put your ear to the ground, you could hear dead warriors talking with their wives and children. Frankly, I never dared put my ear to the ground. Terror at night, though, was a splendid antidote to the lassitude of hot August afternoons for a boy freelancing with a hoe and earning a dime an hour.

Often I spent weeks on the farm of my Swedish-immigrant grandparents, especially when my mother was having yet another baby. I walked down long rows of corn twice my height, through wheat fields, often ending up near a pond where the white bones of slaughtered cattle and pigs were dumped and mammoth water snakes glided across the sheen of algae on the water. If there was rain or a thunderstorm, I sat in the Model A or under an upended pig-scalding pot on sawhorses, listening to what my brother said was Chinese music. In the barn I sat on a milk stool and listened to the cattle and draft horses eating in the dark, or up in the mow I could lie back in the hay with all the barn cats, uncatchable in the daylight, surrounding me at night like true friends.

It is amusing to think that the God I thought had ruptured my eyeball and propelled me into the dark is now, evidently, a mascot of the Republican party. Times change.

I remember slipping out of the farmhouse and walking three miles across the fields to a small village by a lake, where there was a roller-skating rink, roofed but with sides open to the night air. Girls in dresses as brief as bathing suits would float around and around to improbably beautiful organ music. When the girls stopped for a rest, they would chatter and brush back their damp hair. Standing by the railing, I thought they all looked and smelled very good. I would move as close as courage allowed, exposing the uninjured side of my face and hoping to be noticed. I was always bumping into things, what with missing the whole left side of the world.

My father, as the county agricultural agent, helped run the annual fair. It was basically an exposition and competition of farm animals and produce, with the highlights being a horse pulling contest and a 4-H amateur talent show. Along with the last day of school, after which my failings would no longer be noticed for three months, the fair was the main event of the year. I never managed my behavior very well, then or now. One evening I ate cotton candy, hot dogs, french fries, drank a half dozen pops at a nickel a bottle and smoked a filched cigar. For some reason I became ill and walked off into the dark beyond the parked cars and stock trucks, up a long slope and through a field of oats to an elm tree, where I lay down and puked my heart out. When I recovered and looked back down the hill at the fair, it was a wildly colored and beautiful jewel: the gold, vertical bracelet of the Ferris wheel, the smell of the cattle and horse barns, the merry-go-round music, the racked machinery of the tilt-a-whirl, and from a stage in front of the bleachers, a blond girl I favored sang "Candy Kisses," followed by a man playing "The Old Rugged Cross" on a musical handsaw.

We are more equal at night. At nineteen, in New York City and San Francisco, I admired Ginsberg's "Howl" and wanted to be among the "best minds of my generation destroyed by madness, starving hysterical naked/ dragging themselves through the negro streets at dawn looking for an angry fix." I wasn't quite sure how to go about it, but I tried, crisscrossing both cities, discovering garlic and Benzedrine, playing the music I loved in my head—Charlie Parker, Stravinsky, Thelonious Monk, George Shearing, Telemann, Sonny Rollins. Later there were night walks in Paris and London, Costa Rica and Ecuador, where I flushed a tree full of vultures on a cliff far above the Pacific swells; Moscow and Leningrad, where I walked the Neva embankment, thinking about my distant cousin, the poet Sergei Yesenin; the beach north of Mombasa, where tiny, finger-size poisonous snakes tried to get in my pant cuffs; Rio, where you can store minuscule bikinis in your cheeks like a Buddha squirrel. Foreign oceans have the aura of countries that cartographers have forgotten to put on maps.

At present I have tried to stop everything, pure and simple, stuffing time and memory into a custom-blown fishbowl from Belgium, but without success. At my cabin, miles from the nearest neighbor in the Upper Peninsula of Michigan, I walk at night when the moon isn't shrouded by the fog or the cold rain that dominates the area—weather that seems to suit my temperament. I hear coyotes, whippoorwills and loons, bears wallowing off through swamps, and once I heard and saw a timber wolf. If you are bored, strained, lacerated, enervated by the way we live now, I suggest a night walk as far as you can get from a trace of civilization. This form of walking is a dance, and the ghost that follows you, your moon-cast shadow, is your true, androgynous parent, bearing within its distinct outline the child who has always directed your every move.

Poems & Fiction

from *The Theory & Practice of Rivers and New Poems*, 1989

Homily

by Jim Harrison

These simple rules to live within—a black
pen at night, a gold pen in daylight,
avoid blue food and ten-ounce shots
of whiskey, don't point a gun at yourself,
don't snipe with the cri-cri-cri of a *becassine*,
don't use gas for starter fluid, don't read
dirty magazines in front of stewardesses—
it happens all the time; it's time to stop
cleaning your plate, forget the birthdays
of the dead, give all you can to the poor.
This might go on and on and will: who can
choose between the animal in the road
and the ditch? A magnum for lunch
is a little too much but not enough
for dinner. Polish the actual stars at night
as an invisible man pets a dog, an actual
man a memory-dog lost under
the morning glory trellis forty years ago.
Dance with yourself with all your heart
and soul, and occasionally others, but don't
eat all the berries birds eat or you'll die.
Kiss yourself in the mirror but don't fall in love
with photos of ladies in magazines. Don't fall
in love as if you were falling through
the floor in an abandoned house, or off
a dock at night, or down a crevasse
covered with false snow, a cow floundering
in quicksand while the other cows watch
without particular interest, backwards

off a crumbling cornice. Don't fall in love
with two at once. From the ceiling you can see
this circle of three, though one might be elsewhere.
He is rended, he rends himself, he dances,
he whirls so hard everything he *is* flies off.
He crumples as paper but rises daily from the dead.

Porpoise

by Jim Harrison

Every year, when we're fly fishing for tarpon
off Key West, Guy insists that porpoises
are good luck. But it's not so banal
as catching more fish or having a fashion
model fall out of the sky lightly on your head,
or at your feet depending on certain
preferences. It's what porpoises do to the ocean.
You see a school making love off Boca Grande,
the baby with his question mark staring
at us a few feet from the boat.
Porpoises dance for as long as they live.
You can do nothing for them.
They alter the universe.

Counting Birds

by Jim Harrison

As a child, fresh out of the hospital
with tape covering the left side
of my face, I began to count birds.
At age fifty the sum total is precise
and astonishing, my only secret.
Some men count women or the cars
they've owned, their shirts—
long sleeved and short sleeved—
or shoes, but I have my birds,
excluding, of course, those extraordinary
days: the twenty-one thousand
snow geese and sandhill cranes at
Bosque del Apache; the sky blinded
by great frigate birds in the Pacific
off Anconcito, Ecuador; the twenty-one
thousand pink flamingos in Ngorongoro Crater
in Tanzania; the vast flock of sea birds
on the Seri coast of the Sea of Cortez
down in Sonora that left at nightfall,
then reappeared, resuming
their exact positions at dawn;
the one thousand cliff swallows nesting
in the sand cliffs of Pyramid Point,
their small round burrows like eyes,
really the souls of the Anasazi who flew
here a thousand years ago
to wait the coming of the Manitou.
And then there were the usual, almost deadly
birds of the soul—the crow with silver
harness I rode one night as if she
were a black, feathered angel;
the birds I became to escape unfortunate

circumstances—how the skin ached
as the feathers shot out toward light;
the thousand birds the dogs helped
me shoot to become a bird (grouse, woodcock,
duck, dove, snipe, pheasant, prairie chicken, etc.).
On my deathbed I'll write this secret
number on a slip of paper and pass
it to my wife and two daughters.
It will be a hot evening in late June
and they might be glancing out the window
at the thunderstorm's approach from the west.
Looking past their eyes and a dead fly
on the window screen I'll wonder
if there's a bird waiting for me in the onrushing
clouds.
O birds, I'll sing to myself, you've carried
me along on this bloody voyage,
carry me now into that cloud,
into the marvel of this final night.

KEITH WILSON

Keith Wilson (1927–2009) was born in Clovis, New Mexico, attended the US Naval Academy, and served three tours of duty as a much-decorated lieutenant in the Korean War. He returned to receive a graduate degree at the University of New Mexico and taught at the universities of Arizona and Nevada, Reno. His many awards and fellowships include the National Endowment for the Arts.

My father, who had published some of Keith's work in *Sumac*, suggested we publish *Graves Registry*, and put us in touch. Wilson defined the title as a "Joint Service Operation that comes in after battles, and wars, to count the dead, identify bones, draw up a total of what has been lost." Russell, in the later Clark City years with Sally Epps, also put out the monumental *Shaman of the Desert: The Collected Poems 1965–2001* (2009).

A point of pride—Keith Wilson regarded *Graves Registry*, which Stacy Sandler and I helped Anne Garner design, as his finest work.

from *Graves Registry*, 1992

XIV
Waterfront Bars

by Keith Wilson

& how they look—from the sea
the neon glitter softens, grows
warm

—a man can almost smell
beer, women

From Beppu, on the Inland Sea,
the giant "Asahi" beersign stood
steady as any navigational light

drew, caught
attention: we, sailing by
returned to seadamp bunks
strong coffee

3 months on service duty ahead
north of the bombline &
then back we came, wondering

—lights of Yokosuka, Sasebo
Yokohama. We sailed to them
each in turn. Worlds brushed,
passed

each in turn.

—leaving the darkness of night
watches, silver turning of screws,
wake piled high behind
the blackened ship: little pieces
of a man, left here, there.

CXXII
A School of Small Fish

by Keith Wilson

swimming in a radiant
bluegreen circle of flashing
tiny hardly born wiggles

all those little jaws
following the drowning man
down helpless before his size
his tough tough skin

CXXIII
The Trey of Spades

by Keith Wilson

Somehow another language
always sounds sweeter than
our own

                    Romanian, French,
German, Latin, old dreams
of what we might have been

while a Fool remains a card
in a deck of cards, never answers
for the long long years

or for what we have come to be
in our own tongues we speak
those few hidden words
that whisper of what we seek

I speak now of Paris, tritely, without sense
of what it may have meant to you, or you, and
only of those few nights caught in longing,
hovering about the thighs of that girl
who shared my friend's bed when I slept alone,
a borne scent on a city's heavy breath
—those lights, neon gauze shading
a vision that permitted no lies, no
endless sequence of permissibility.

Paris, Paris, she was dead before I found her.
Blew like a pale leaf through the stars.

GREG KEELER

Greg Keeler (1946–) is a poet, songwriter, artist, and humorist who has taught creative writing and English literature at Montana State University since 1975. A recipient of the Governor's Award for Excellence, he's the author of six books (including *Waltzing with the Captain: Remembering Richard Brautigan*), several chapbooks, and numerous plays and songs. His poems have received praise from Gary Snyder, Edward Dorn, Tim Cahill, and David Quammen, who calls them "lunatic masterpieces." He is very tall, but quite shy, and he lives in Bozeman, Montana.

from *Epiphany at Goofy's Gas*, 1991

Salmon Fly Hatch on the Henry's Fork

by Greg Keeler

A whistle like grass-wind
and sun off a swan's back
stings the Tetons sharper
than blue. Salmon fly

sputters the weather woven
into her wings down the
Henry's Fork and through the
webbed water. Moon says

now, lasting into her
daytime reflection on clear
water and longer as if the
thick hatch were all there

were of night. And the
amplified day: rainbows
perking then rippling the
water into circles then

breaking those circles.
Grass bends the banks down
farther then farther with
the weight of the hatch.

There's so much reflected
here. There's so much to
be shattered then smooth
then shattered into those

clear shards that only trout
can remember and even they
are a memory under the whistle
and glare. Reflections

of swans and the Tetons will
start it again and again
in the green-early years. The
rock-bottom, glass-water years.

The Ghost of Richard Brautigan on Trail Creek

by Greg Keeler

Trail Creek where?
And what was he using?
Flies tied from
spun diamond?
Did he know the algebra
of the stones?
Was his hair its
usual silly gold?
Did he fall and fill
his purple polka-dot
waders? Did his words
hover over the pools
like clouds of midges?
No?
Then there's
still hope.

DAN GERBER

Dan Gerber (1940–), whom Annie Dillard called "one of our finest living poets," made the transition from a man of action to a man of letters at high speed, after hitting a wall at Altamont in 1966. He became the publisher of the literary journal *Sumac*, with Jim Harrison, whom he'd met in the early sixties at Michigan State University; he was much more disciplined in dealing with the piles of manuscripts than his coeditor. He published three books with Clark City: a short-story collection named *Grass Fires* (one of the most beautiful books the press produced), the lauded novel *A Voice from the River*, which garnered praise from Robert F. Jones and Charles Baxter, and the poetry collection *A Last Bridge Home*. Beyond being one of my favorite humans since the time we met at Stony Brook in 1968, he was a friend to the press, keeping it alive financially and bolstering Russell's morale. And he was certainly the sanest of the crew.

Why I Don't Take Naps in the Afternoon

from *A Last Bridge Home: New and Selected Poems*, 1992
by Dan Gerber

It occurs to you that everything has gone awry.
It all should have turned out differently.
Everyone has chosen the wrong mate. Everything
that should have been spoken has been restrained.
It's not the world but the residue of what the
world intended. It all makes sense to you, now
that your mistresses have gotten married. Eternity.
We are living in eternity.

The clouds break open, the sun about to set.
Nothing you can do about it. You walk from your
hotel, down rain-washed streets, glistening in places.
The cafés are closed, or you feel they should
be closed. The life in them doesn't concern you.
Exhausted by certainty, nothing concerns you
but the pull of the river, the dark
brown current swirling in eddies, drawn too
powerfully to what it doesn't know, not to turn
back on itself. You watch a glassy ring, watch it
ripple then curl, till it's lost in the stream.
And you notice the pavement under your feet, the
hardness of it, and of the iron rail under your arms.

from

A Voice from the River

by Dan Gerber, 1990

SOMETIMES WEEKS WOULD GO BY without Russell's giving a thought to the spot near the corner of Ottawa and Main, a spot he passed almost every day on his way to the office, where his great-grandfather had been hanged.

According to J.M. Leet's *Early Days of Wing County* (set down in green buckram on typed onionskin), Ambrose Wheeler had been strung up by an angry mob on a raw October evening in 1880 for a murder he didn't commit. It had been a shameful episode for the settlers and their immediate issue, but the passing of a century made it a legend, a distinction comparable to Greencastle, Indiana's veiled pride in having a bank once robbed by John Dillinger.

Russell held no grudge against the people of Five Oaks. As a boy, when he and his buddies had played at being the Youngers or the James Gang, he'd enjoyed being able to say that his own great-grandfather had been the last man known to have been hanged in the county. It had given his outlawry a halo of authenticity. Later, as the town's largest employer, it provided a common touch.

According to Russell's father, Daniel, Great-Granddaddy Ambrose had probably needed hanging, if not for the murder of his mistress, Mrs. Tredwell Johnston, then for an accumulation of transgressions going back to his days as a captain in Wesley Merritt's cavalry, harassing Mosby's Confederacy east of the Shenandoah Valley.

In fighting Mosby's raiders, it was said that Ambrose had become so adept as a guerrilla fighter that he'd continued his forays on the defeated South long after Appomattox, and become wealthy in the process. How else could he have lived the way he did, built his big house, gambled, whored and become creditor (so the family believed, though Leet didn't mention it), to half the crowd who lynched him? He had come home almost a year later than the other men of Five Oaks with a chestful of medals, and had done little to dispel stories that he had personally killed over a hundred Confederates and that his company had taken no prisoners.

The lynch mob, led by Tredwell Johnston himself, took its revenge fifteen years after the war when the luster on Ambrose's medals had tarnished. The resentment of those veterans who had fought with small glory in the 5th Michigan Infantry had been inflamed by gambling debts owed Ambrose, and they conveniently rekindled their ire with the conviction that he had not fought out of any sense of patriotism or for the preservation of the Union, but purely for adventure and profit. The real killer was apprehended a week later when he tried to pawn off a gold brooch on Johnny Puff, a whoring buddy of Ambrose's. The brooch was known by Puff to have been given to Pauline Johnston by Ambrose himself. Mr. Johnston, doubly grieved, apologized to the Widow Wheeler and her infant son, Cyrus, on behalf of the people of Five Oaks. They gave her the brooch and $230 in gold and called it even.

Russell often wondered how this supposedly desperate character had fathered a line of stolid businessmen, so-called pillars of the community. Had the family unconsciously (or consciously) been trying to atone for this aberration in its heritage? Or had Ambrose simply been given as bad a rap on his whole life story as on the episode which had brought it to an early end? Russell wondered if there were any living descendants of Jesse James and, if so, how they now regarded their notorious ancestor.

Obviously there had been some basis for the town's feelings about Ambrose in those years following the Civil War. Russell had evidence of this in Ambrose's pistol, an 1851, .36 caliber Colt Navy, on the butt of which there were six carved notches. That the pistol had been handed down to Russell through three generations suggested that Ambrose's memory had been considered worth preserving. The pistol had come into Russell's hands when his grandfather died. His father apparently hadn't cared about possessing it. Russell didn't know why, and he wondered at what point he would pass on to Nick this tainted Excalibur of the Wheeler succession. Considering the lackluster lives which had followed Ambrose's, his was a myth worth fostering.

Occasionally Russell took the revolver down from its dark perch above the cornice of his den wall. He would appreciate the surprising heft of it, half cock it and savor the click of the spinning cylinder, full cock it and aim through the sight on the lip of the hammer and then ease back the spring. Finally he would contemplate the six crudely carved notches in the handle, now whitening with age and with the residue of brass polish he used on the backstrap. There was a story there, or six stories. Of course it was possible that Ambrose had never shot anyone, that he had notched his pistol purely for effect, though Russell doubted it when he considered the authenticity of the rope stretched out by the weight of his great-grandfather's body.

Yard Sale

from *Grass Fires*, 1989
by Dan Gerber

I DON'T THINK there's anything prettier than west Michigan this time of May. Dogwood, lilacs, apple blossoms against the undarkened green of new leaves and new grass. I thought about that driving in to work this morning. Alice was having a yard sale, and I had Saturday E.R. duty. I don't like yard sales. They've always seemed to me like airing your dirty laundry. All the cast-off debris of people's lives laid out on tables to be picked over by anyone who's curious. I never liked going to them, and I argued against having this one, but Alice runs the house and has her way. She says it's just because I'm a Pisces. I'll put empty toothpaste tubes back in the medicine cabinet, and she'll go through and clean them out, replace my worn-out toothbrushes and restock. I can't argue with her. But to see all those old things put together on display—bicycles, roller skates, Ray Jr.'s baseball shoes—a picture of what we aren't anymore. I worried about Alice's handling the empty nest, the kids grown and gone, but I guess I'm the one.

Jill's married and works for IBM in Cincinnati, and Ray Jr.'s in his third year of law school. I'm proud of them both, but sometimes I don't know what I'm doing anymore. I've been a doctor almost thirty years now, and it isn't what I thought it would be. I had some idea about being the country doctor when I came here from Detroit. A kind of missionary. I'm not religious, I don't mean that, but they were desperate here, and I chose it over catching babies in Bloomfield Hills. I would bring good medicine to the sticks. But this isn't the sticks. It's a place, a good place, and when I go back to Detroit, that's what seems strange to me.

But it's never gotten any easier to tell someone they're dying or to tell their husband or their wife or their children. I thought I'd grow into these things. But how do you tell a man that his daughter you've treated all her life has died of something people just don't die of? It was like some kind of tasteless joke. I did everything that was indicated, but she didn't respond. I gave her oxygen and an I.V. to rehydrate her. I put her on aminophylline and adrenalin, an I.P.P.B. I intubated her, and nothing worked.

She was a friend of my daughter's when they were in school. She spent weekends at our house, and she and Jill would put on plays in the basement and charge us a quarter admission. She would giggle before every line and then pull herself in and deliver it beautifully and then giggle again at the very idea that she had actually said something like, "Oh Oswald, you are the source of all my woe."

I remember that because it was the last line she said before the power went out. It had been thundering outside and they finished the play by candlelight. Ray Jr., who was younger than the girls, played all the bit parts. "Now I'm the raven; now I'm the messenger; now I'm the tall pine tree," they would have him say. Jill directed and kept the show going. "Now be serious," she would say. But when she got past her giggles, Nancy was what kept our interest. She said her lines like she believed them, and she made us believe them too. She brought me close to tears a couple of times. They were silly little plays the kids had made up, but sometimes Nancy would take off with a speech that hadn't been planned. She'd see something or feel something and talk about the ring of trees where she was to meet her prince, how she would go there every night till the end of time, even though he never returned from the Crusades. Nancy could have read the telephone book and made us cry.

Jill went off to college, and Nancy got married right out of high school. We predicted it wouldn't work, and it didn't. She had a baby, a little girl, and six months later her husband went to California. He got work with a company that built greenhouses. He sent money back, child support, and a year after that, he married again.

And today Nancy died in the emergency room. I'd read of patients dying of asthma attacks. I'd read of people dying of measles, but you don't expect to see it in a small town E.R. You expect cardiacs and farm and highway accidents, drownings in the summer, gunshot wounds in the fall. But you don't expect a beautiful young woman with a six-year-old daughter to suffocate in your arms on what might have been the prettiest day of the year. I felt betrayed. I felt Nancy had done this to me, that she was being dramatic, that she had made it all up. She was crying and pleading with me not to let her die. "My little girl," she gasped out in that horrible wheezing voice, those faint words squeezed out from the back of the throat. "Nancy, you're okay," I said. I stroked her hair. "Relax and your breath will come back." I knew I could save her. I'd been through this same kind of thing a hundred times before. But she didn't relax, and her breath didn't come back, and I went into a rage. "Nancy, God damn it! Don't do this!" I pounded the gurney with my fist. I shook her. I cried. I threw my stethoscope across the room. The nurses and orderlies were embarrassed for me. They shrank back out of the way as if they thought I might hit someone. I walked to the doctors' lounge, and I closed the door. I couldn't talk to Bob Russell. If she'd been in a car crash and bled to death, I could have handled it. I could've said, "We did everything we could."

Yesterday when I was helping Alice get ready for her yard sale, she brought something down from the attic, something I didn't know we even owned, something I didn't want to see. It was a hassock, flat on top and sewn in triangles of leather on the sides so that it resembled a snare drum. It had been my father's footstool in our house in Ferndale when I was a child. It must be the same one. I can't imagine we would've found another one like it, or if we had, that I would have let Alice buy it. I don't know how it could have ended up in our attic. It was the stool that had sat in front of my father's morris chair. My father would come home from work at G.M. and plop down in the chair and put his feet on that hassock, and that's where he lived. My memories of my father are almost exclusively memories of him sitting in that chair. Sometimes when he was at work and I'd come home from school, I'd look at the chair and see how his body had broken it down to a mold, a negative image. Several times I tried the chair, but it just wasn't comfortable. I would get up right away with a feeling I'd done something wrong.

But the hassock held its shape. For all the years his feet rested on it, it stayed flat on top. Maybe he hadn't had it as long as he'd had the chair. I don't know. He and my mother had been married ten years before I came along, and the chair and the hassock were there.

My father died in that chair. I found him in it one spring morning when I got up to read the Sunday comics. He'd been working on our travel-trailer in the driveway a few days earlier, when it slipped on the jacks and an axle bumped his head. He seemed to be all right at first, but something had changed. He looked funny, and he was quiet. I was only ten, and I thought he was angry. On that Saturday morning he hit my sister because she had been late getting home from a date Friday night. I'd never seen a grown-up hit anyone before. Neither he nor my mother had ever hit me. Mother stepped in and stopped it. She told us to stay away from him. She said he was sick, and that's why he looked at us the way he did.

Then that Sunday morning I came downstairs. I got the funny papers from the porch and took them to the living room. At first I thought he was sleeping, that he'd fallen asleep in his chair. But then I saw the blood on his face and his .22 Colt Woodsman on the floor beside him. I don't know why no one had heard the shot. He was sitting there with his eyes open and his head slumped down so that it seemed as if he were looking at the hassock. And then I looked at the hassock and saw that there were three bullets on it, all standing on end in a row. I'll never know, of course, but I thought right then of my sister, my mother and me.

After the funeral, my mother had some men come and get the chair. I don't know what they did with it, but I pushed the hassock back into the corner of the room and covered it with the drapes by the French doors that opened out to the backyard, and I don't remember ever seeing it again until Alice brought it down from the attic.

I thought about the hassock as I sat there in the doctor's lounge, thought of it emerging again now and wondered about all those years between. I thought of the yard sale going on at that moment, of the past being sold off, the bicycles finding new riders, the roller skates new sidewalks, the props and costumes of our basement theater finding new homes, new stories; not people finding things, but things finding new lives. I thought about the things Nancy had used in her life, the English saddle she'd been so proud of, the rag doll called Luka she brought with her when she would come to spend the night.

I heard the nurse calling my name, "Dr. Walsh. Dr. Walsh," but I didn't respond till she put her hand on my shoulder. "Dr. Walsh. Mr. Russell. He's waiting."

I'd never known Bob Russell well. We'd passed a few words years before when he would bring Nancy in to our house to visit Jill or when I would drop Jill off for a weekend on their farm. He was a quiet man, not taciturn as farmers often are, as if they knew something they weren't going to tell you. Bob Russell was just a little bit shy. I found him in the lobby, sitting quietly, looking at his hands, as if in church, waiting for the service to begin. He stood up when he saw me, and he held out his hand. I wanted to say something original. I wanted to talk about the beautiful weather, some way of telling him that wouldn't be painful. It's tough enough just losing a patient. "Bob, I'm sorry," I said. "We did everything we could."

On the way home, I wondered why it couldn't have been raining. It was that one day when the apple trees and flowering crabs are in perfect bloom, and you know it can't last.

I didn't tell Alice about Nancy. I will in time. I'll have to call Jill and tell her. The bicycles had sold, the roller skates, the half-scale electric Model A I'd bought the kids on Jill's twelfth birthday, even Ray Jr.'s baseball shoes. Alice was pleased. Way more than half the stuff she had laid out was gone. But nobody bought the hassock.

"Carrie DeFrees looked at that," Alice told me. "She put it with the rest of her stuff, and then she brought it back. 'Too colonial,' she said."

"I'd kind of hoped this one would go," I said.

"You can take it to the dump if you want to," Alice sighed. She was totaling up her sales on a clipboard. It was the end of a hot afternoon, and I was tired. I sat down on the hassock and looked at the few things that were left: a box of odd buttons, an assortment of cookie cutters, an upright hair dryer, the old push lawn mower I'd used on my parents' yard in Ferndale.

After dinner I helped Alice clean up the yard. I wheeled the lawn mower back to its corner in the tool shed and felt nostalgic about the clatter it made. We folded up the tables and stored them along the wall of the garage, and I carried the hassock back up to the attic. We took a walk around the neighborhood before it got dark.

"It feels like summer," Alice said. "You should get out your video camera and get these blossoms on tape. One good rain and they'll all be gone."

"I will," I said. "I'll do it tomorrow."

RICHARD CURREY

Richard Currey's (1949-) first two books, *Crossing Over* and *Fatal Light*, are both considered to be among the finest literary works to emerge from the Vietnam Era. *Fatal Light* was short-listed for the PEN/Hemingway Award, received the Vietnam Veterans of America's Excellence in the Arts Award, and was published in ten languages. Currey is also a journalist and has written over 50 nonfiction pieces focusing on the intersection of military veterans and health issues. His journalism has contributed to landmark court settlements, major legislation, and federal policy changes that have benefited thousands of veterans. A two-time recipient of National Endowment for the Arts Fellowships, Currey's short stories have won both O. Henry and Pushcart Prizes and been heard on NPR and Sirius XM.

from

Crossing Over: The Vietnam Stories

by Richard Currey, 1993

I HAVE BEEN WALKING a long time. Everything about the forest is glazed and bizarre: trees hanging upside down with dark birds floating in the stark roots like fish. When I look at my feet they are huge and foreign, shapeless black oblongs that are connected to me but I cannot feel, that do not belong to me. The walking pads on, my head drifting weightless above the feet and legs and chest like a helium balloon towed in a parade. I keep feeling a fall is inevitable, a hole or precipice, and I try to stop but there is a distorted, sleepy inertia. The walking goes simply on and the boredom and odd silence collect like heavy fluids in my throat and behind my eyes: it is the kind of dream that runs down under its own gravity and I wake up quietly, cut loose and empty.

Feet over the edge and working my way down the bunks, four of them. My jungle boots unlaced and shuffling: I limp into the head, punch out a handful of water and rub my face. The glance in the mirror before going to a stall. I sit down and see somebody's taped up a picture of a woman fucking herself with a shiny green plastic dildo.

I get out before the fear works on me.

Here are the facts of the matter.

Miguel Maldonado is nineteen years of age, a Lance Corporal in the United States Marine Corps, a first-generation Cuban-American from Miami, Florida. He is smart, funny, courageous. A high-school dropout who speaks with a strong Spanish accent, he is a former regional Golden Gloves finalist and holds the Purple Heart, the Bronze Star, and several unit commendations and battle stars. He has, on more than one occasion, saved the lives of his fellow marines and platoon commander. He gets on with everybody in his unit, no matter their backgrounds, prejudices, religion, or politics. He has a natural inclination toward excellence: a soldier's soldier. He speaks of a career in the Marine Corps, telling everyone he has found a home at last. He is astonished to find himself successful and, despite the stress of combat, he is a happy man. It is in the last days of 1968 that Maldonado loses his right leg at mid-thigh and I use his belt as a crude tourniquet in the minutes before he is airlifted to the Naval Hospital at Cam Ranh Bay. When I see him next it is by chance, having escorted two wounded marines into the same hospital. There has been some trouble with the leg—a sloppy amputation, an infection—and Maldonado is medically addicted to opiates of one form or another. The bright energy and wide-eyed courage are gone. Maldonado knows he has entered the next stage of his life: a disabled Cuban high-school dropout drug addict, without prospects or direction. I sit with him beside his bed. When I rise to go he grips my wrist. After a moment, however, he drops his hand. I say good-bye, wish him well, but he does not answer or look at me.

Here are the facts of the matter.

What we see and know will live forever in this snapping light in the eyes, the mouth shaping one question after another, the voice sounding one question after another, the piracy of time saying *I can go no further than this. It is unsafe to go further than this.* Flowing back into the blank hard eye of a soldier's one job, this last freedom failing into the heart, never fully knowing how far you can go if called to the task, how long the darkness is or how far above your head it extends, how long you might walk before the earth gives way in a watery lost moment, knowing the soldier's one job is not a complicated affair: locate the enemy and, having done so, destroy that enemy by any means available before the same intention is visited from the opposite direction. It is a game of sorts, a contest, winners taking nothing in this elaborate boy's contest taken to the limit of imagination and current possibility. Look around: the jungle sings. The insects and snakes and hardwoods breathe, and I can nearly believe they know we are here, sense our passage and find us ridiculous, transitory, at odds with existence, objects suitable only for pity. The sky reaches ground in patches, its weight giving root to the forest floor we cross, the forest a book we cannot read, legs moving against it, insect rattle, hollow monkey bone. I could conjure an entire magic out of this forest floor, braising dead leaves and mud between the palms, chanting under my breath *monkey bone take me home, take me home, take me home*

RUSSELL CHATHAM

Grass Fires

1989, oil on canvas, 20″×16″

One Hundred Paintings, 1990

Dusk

1975, oil on canvas, 30″×35″

Russell Chatham, 1987

October

1985, lithograph, 34″×45″

Missouri Headwaters, 1986

Livingston, Montana, home of Clark City Press (© Stephen Collector)

The Sporting Club (from left): Guy de la Valdène, Jim Harrison, Thomas McGuane, and Russell Chatham in Key West in 1988 (© Stephen Collector)

STEPHEN COLLECTOR

Walter Feuz was born June 12, 1911, near Driggs, Idaho, and grew up on a 160-acre homestead on Spread Creek, east of Moran Junction, Wyoming, where this portrait was taken in May of 1986.

The Law of the Range: Portraits of Old-Time Brand Inspectors, 1991

PETER STACKPOLE

Tennis star Eleanor Cushingham uses Raymond Loewy's Palm Springs solarium, 1947.

Peter Stackpole: Life in Hollywood, 1936-1952, 1992

DIANA GUEST

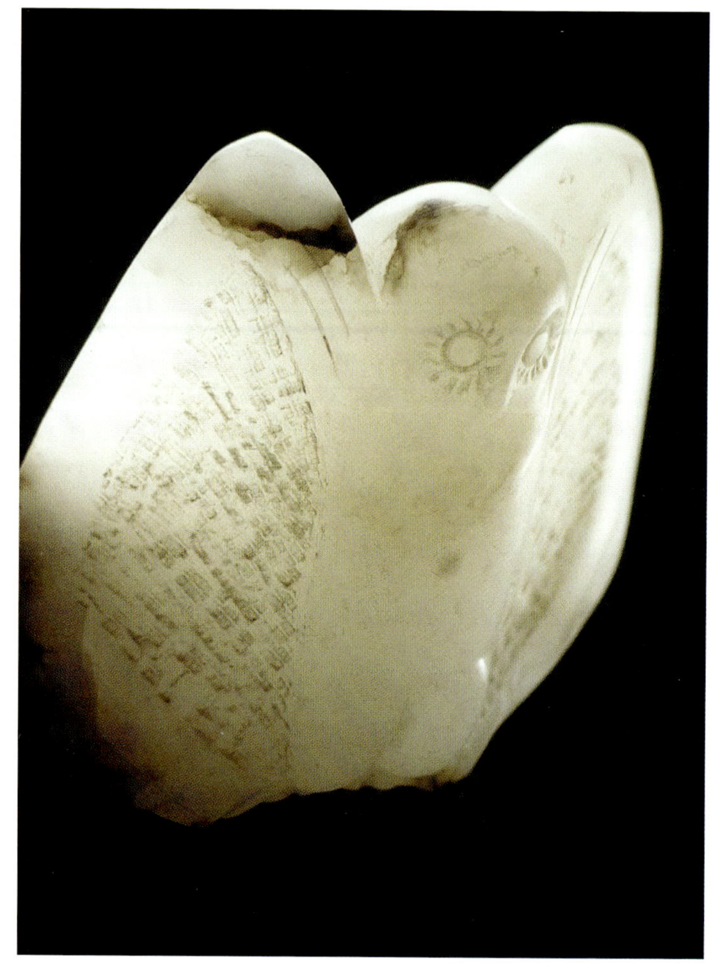

Hovering Owl

alabaster, 6½"×13½"×13"

Stonecarver, 1993

BARRY GIFFORD

Barry Gifford (1946–), the author of *Wild at Heart* (filmed by David Lynch), *Sailor's Holiday*, and *The Devil Thumbs a Ride*, has received awards from PEN, the NEA, and the ALA. *A Good Man to Know* was described by the New Orleans *Times-Picayune* as "a striking collection of minimalist personal essays, each as finely wrought as a hand-cut diamond." *The New York Times* described *New Mysteries of Paris* as "not simply innovative; it achieves a subtle, penetrating clarity." And then we have Andrew Vachss, who said that Gifford's writing "makes Camus look like Pollyanna."

He's a raconteur, and a joy to work with. His happiness at Russell's manic decision to hold a Clark City reading at Books & Co. in Manhattan, and to put his authors up at the Carlyle, was catching, even as the bills landed.

My Mother's People

from *A Good Man to Know: A Semi-Documentary Fictional Memoir*, 1992
by Barry Gifford

MY FATHER was Jewish, he died when I was twelve, and soon after the funeral my mother—she and my father had been divorced since I was five—was approached by my father's family who told her that the least she could do was to have me bar-mitzvahed. "For Rudolph's sake," Esther, my father's sister, said. "He would have wanted his son to be bar-mitzvahed."

She knew as well as I and my mother that Rudolph had not been at all religious. In fact, he had almost been ostracized by his family for marrying my mother, a Catholic. The marriage had not worked out because of family interference, mainly by my mother's mother, who didn't want her twenty-two-year-old daughter (my father was fifteen years older) running around with gangsters.

That part of it was true. My father ran an all-night liquor store on the corner of Chicago and Rush, next door to the Club Alabam where I used to watch the show girls rehearse on Saturday afternoons. I often ate breakfast at the small lunch counter in the store, dunking doughnuts with the organ-grinder's monkey. Big redheaded Louise ran the counter and fed me milk shakes while I waited for my dad. The place was a drop joint for stolen goods, dope, whatever somebody wanted to stash for a while. The story was that you could get anything at the store day or night. I used to see my dad giving guys penicillin shots in the basement, and I remember my mother throwing a fit when I was four years old sitting at three in the morning on a bundle of newspapers playing with a gun Bill Moore, a private cop, had given me to look at.

This kind of thing spooked my mother. My dad wore black shirts and gold ties, spoke with "dese" and "dose" and was famous for knocking guys through plate-glass windows. He'd done it twice—once in the newspaper the next day he'd been described as "that well-known man-about-town." Al Capone's brother, who was then using the name White, would come into the store often, as well as movie star Dorothy Lamour, ex-middleweight champ Tony Zale (who had a restaurant across the street—he used to show me the gloves from his matches), and whoever else was in town. We lived on Chestnut Street, next to the lake, in the Seneca Hotel, which was later described to me as containing "the lobby of the men with no last names."

My grandmother's fears were not unfounded. At one point, while my mother and father were vacationing in Hawaii, my dad received a phone call telling him somebody had been shot and that it would be best for them to extend their holiday. That was the first six-month absence of which I was aware. Later my parents spent a few months as the guest of Johnny Reata in Jamaica during another cooling-off period. Reata, my mother told me, had made his money running guns to Trujillo in the Dominican Republic.

While my mother, being a former University of Texas beauty queen, enjoyed the high-life aspects of being married to my father, the hoodlum end of it, plus the great influence her mother had over her, forced her to leave him, and I moved with her to the far North Side of the city. I continued to see my dad regularly until he died, and at no time did he ever so much as point out to me what a synagogue looked like, let alone tell me that he wanted me to be bar-mitzvahed.

For some reason my mother allowed herself to be influenced by my Aunt Esther and my dad's brother Bruno, both of whom were hypocritical Jews. Neither they, nor my Uncle Joel, Esther's husband, who also interceded on my deceased father's behalf, and who once told me, looking me straight in the eye, that deep down inside 95 percent of the Gentiles hate the Jews and could not be trusted—including me, he meant, because of my mother—went to the synagogue except for High Holiday services; social appearances. They were stingy, mean, conniving people who had always been envious of my mother's good looks and power over my father, resenting the fact that my father had ever married her.

What made it so important that I be bar-mitzvahed, they told my mother, was that I was the first son in the family. Both Bruno and Esther had had two girls apiece. I was the first one eligible to carry on the family name and tradition. And my father's father, the old man, my grandfather Ezra, who used to run numbers from his candy stand under the Addison Street el, was still alive. For his sake, before he passed away, they whined to my mother, I should be bar-mitzvahed.

So my mother was persuaded. Her mother had died a few years before so there was no one to whom she could go for advice. I had to take Hebrew lessons. Three days a week after school I would sit with a little man who smelled of smoked fish, who spoke almost no English, and memorize words I did not understand. I also went to the synagogue each Saturday morning for nearly a year after my father died to say a prayer for him. My father's family insisted that I go, even though I had never been inside a synagogue before in my life. This was necessary, it was a son's duty, they explained, and my mother reluctantly acceded to their wishes. So on Saturdays I stood at the back of the temple, put on a black skullcap and recited a prayer written in English next to the Hebrew on a little pink card.

As the bar-mitzvah day came closer I thought more and more about it, about why I was having to do this. Several times I told my mother I wouldn't go to Hebrew lessons anymore. None of it made sense to me, it was stupid, the whole thing was ridiculous. She knew I was right, but she told me to go through with it. "For your father's sake," she said. "My father's dead," I told her. "It doesn't matter to him and it wouldn't matter to him if he were alive."

But she said to finish it, then the debt to the family would be paid. This reasoning escaped me—I didn't see what we owed to them in the first place. But I stuck it out, and vowed that it really would be the end of it, that no one would ever make me do anything again.

After the bar-mitzvah, which ritual I performed like an automaton, mouthing the lines as if I weren't really there, weren't the one doing it at all, I did not see a member of my father's family—except briefly when my grandfather died—for seven years.

Passing through town those seven years later I went to see my dad's brother. Like my father, Uncle Bruno was a strong-willed, stubborn man. He had done well financially and kept his large brown brick house locked up like a fortress. When he saw me through the front-door window he motioned for me to come around the back way. "Too many bolts to undo in the front," he explained, as he and his wife admitted me through the rear entrance. They expressed their surprise at my being there, they hadn't recognized me right away. I told them I'd just come by to say hello, that was all.

Uncle Bruno insisted that I eat with them, they were just sitting down to dinner, which I did, and tell them what I'd been doing the past few years. I gave them a brief history after which Uncle Bruno asked me if I'd come to see him about a job, or did I need money?

"I don't need any money," I told him, "and I have a job. I'm a writer," I said. My uncle looked annoyed and got up and walked into the living room and sat down. I followed him in and stood by the window. "Why did you come here then, if you don't need any money?" he asked. "Out of curiosity," I said. Bruno lit a cigar. "Curious about what?" he said.

"Do you think things would have been different with me had my father lived?" I asked. "Of course they would," Bruno said. "You would have been a doctor or a lawyer or a pharmacist. Something important."

I knew it bothered Uncle Bruno that I didn't want any money, or anything else, from him. It would have bothered him had I asked for something but at least then he would have had the satisfaction of being right.

"Then I'm glad he died when he did," I said, "before we had any trouble about it."

"Being a Jew means nothing to you, does it?" said Uncle Bruno. "You're one of your mother's people."

I realized I had no reason to be there, that I should never have come. I put on my jacket.

"What did you expect?" I said, and left.

from

New Mysteries of Paris

by Barry Gifford, 1991

NADJA WAS TAKEN to a madhouse in 1928. Someplace in the French countryside where ordinary people, those fortunate enough to have escaped scrutiny, who have avoided so far in their lives being similarly judged and sentenced and dismissed from the greater society, will not be reminded of their own failings by the screams of the outcast.

It is reasonable to suppose that by that time there could not be much difference for Nadja between the inside of a sanitarium and the outside—but Nadja was here, she left something of herself. Certainly she's dead by now, buried in a field behind an insane asylum, cats screwing on her grave.

The day she threatened to jump from the window of her room in the Hotel Sphinx on the Boulevard Magenta I should have known she was not a fake. Who can tell the genuine mad from the fake? Nadja could. She was always pointing them out to me. In a café she'd whisper, "Look at her. Biting her nails. Pretending to be waiting for someone. She's a fake. Her lovers disappear." "But how can you tell?" I'd ask. "Look at my eyes," Nadja would say. "Can you see the way they are lit from behind? I'm dangerous. To be avoided."

Who was Nadja? What was the significance of Nadja in my life? Why does she return, a constant, though I've not seen nor heard of or from her in fifty years?

I saw a woman in a marketplace in a Mexican city, Mérida, perhaps, in the Yucatán, twenty years ago or so. She resembled Nadja, or what she might have looked like, according to my idea of Nadja had she still been alive, let alone an inhabitant of a jungle town in Mexico. I followed her as she moved from stand to stand, inspecting the fruits, dresses, beads, kitchen knives, crucifixes. Was this a woman or a phantom? Her gray hair was worn long and thick and fell across her face so that her features were indistinct, shadowed. Nadja had been blonde, with the short, curled haircut of the day, a brief nose, sharp black hawk's eyes, a long mouth with slender lips, purple, that grinned in one corner only. This hag in the marketplace was fat, toothless, I would say, judging by the line of her jaw, dark-skinned. Nadja had been white as the full moon of February over Venice, almost emaciated, seldom ate, with a full mouth of teeth, crooked but strong. She was capable of cracking open with ease in one swift bite a stalk of Haitian sugarcane.

How could I imagine this hideous, crumbling jungle creature to be Nadja? Some feeling made me follow until, crossing a busy street, I lost sight of her. I panicked and looked around wildly. She was gone and I was forced to suppress a great scream of pain. Unused to this severe sort of anxiety, I battled to control my emotions, there in the midst of a crowd of Indians.

It was what Nadja had meant when she stuck her tongue into my ear as we rode in a cab along the Boulevard Raspail. As quickly as she'd done it she withdrew to the opposite corner of the seat and said, staring blankly ahead, "To me nothing is more terrifying than the curse of self-fulfillment."

What did Nadja do before we met? I asked her many times and mostly she would avoid answering by laughing and kissing me, adjusting my tie or brushing my lapels. She did tell me she was born in Belgium, near Ghent, and that her father raised flowers. She went to the local school, in a convent, and moved to Paris when she was seventeen. She met a man, unidentified, got married, gave birth to a daughter, who promptly died of pneumonia. Those were facts, according to Nadja. The man was gone soon after the daughter.

Other than that there was little Nadja would admit. None of it was important, she said. "Not to you!" She instructed me to invent her story, as it was all the same, unrelated to today. "Who is the hero of a film that has at its center a peacock flying through and landing in the snow?" Nadja asks, licking my chin as if she were here.

RICHARD HUGO

Richard Hugo (1923–1982) grew up outside of Seattle, served as a bombardier over the Mediterranean in World War II, and went to the University of Washington through the GI Bill, where he studied under Theodore Roethke. He came to the University of Montana after *A Run of Jacks* and ended up running the creative writing program, where he taught a generation of Montana writers, including James Welch (*Winter in the Blood*, *Riding the Earthboy 40*, *Fools Crow*), whose wife, Lois Welch, would eventually succeed Hugo as the director of the program.

I knew Hugo's poetry (*Selected Poems*, *What Thou Lovest Well, Remains American*, *The Lady in Kicking Horse Reservoir*) growing up and read his classic *The Triggering Town* in college, but *Death and the Good Life* was handed to me by my friend Peter Lewis (who also got me into Swedish mysteries and P. G. Wodehouse) when we lived together in Brooklyn in the mid-eighties. You just don't forget writing like that, or a woman with an axe; *Death*, along with William Hjortsberg's *Falling Angel*, made me want to write mysteries. Reprinting Hugo's only novel was a cause as soon as Russell said he wanted to publish books. Jim and Lois Welch introduced me to their friend Ripley Hugo, Richard Hugo's widow (whose mother Mildred Walker wrote the beautiful *Winter Wheat*), and she agreed to let us republish. As Jim Welch writes in his preface to the Clark City Press edition, Hugo was "a rare true poet," but "the success of *Death and the Good Life* convinced him that he had more mysteries inside him. We'll never know what he might have written. But we do have this one."

from

Death and the Good Life

by Richard Hugo, 1991

I IMAGINE THE three men having a good time. I imagine them singing. We know they'd had beer for breakfast at the Hammers' house, and we know that Lee's sister, Lynn, had served pancakes and ham. By six A.M. they were off to catch the early fishing at Rainbow Lake. It was mid-September, and at our altitude the nights were already cold. Sedge was receding in the lake now that the surface water was cooling, and the big rainbows were coming up. The three men expected to catch fish, and they felt festive.

That's why I imagine them singing on the eleven-mile drive to the lake from Plains. They'd had beer for breakfast, they expected trout and they felt festive. I never checked with Lee Hammer or Robin Tingley afterward to find out if they actually sang on the way.

Lee and Robin told us they took the boat they'd hauled there out from the south shore of the lake. Ralph McCreedy, the third man, wanted to fish from shore. He got too cramped in boats, he had said, and besides, he liked fishing from shore with bobber and worm. So Lee Hammer and Robin Tingley trolled, and Ralph McCreedy made his way east on the south shore until he found a spot he thought looked good. He set up the lightweight folding lawn chair he'd carried, rigged up, baited his hook and cast out. He then sat down comfortably in the lawn chair to watch his red and yellow bobber drift from left to right in the slight wash of wind from the west. The rest of what happened to Ralph McCreedy I imagine, now that the facts are in.

I imagine that around ten A.M., with two rainbows smaller than he'd anticipated, which we found on his stringer, McCreedy was still studying his bobber. The boat with Hammer and Tingley was not in sight. I imagine McCreedy imagined the boat with his two friends was down near the dam at the far-east end of the lake, around the small headland that hid that part of the lake from him.

I imagine McCreedy heard a noise and thought: bear. He looked around but saw nothing that might have made the noise. The sound could have been a snap of a twig or a cottonwood leaf cracking underfoot. I imagine he heard it a second time and turned again, and again saw nothing.

I imagine the last time he turned he must have been terrified to see the enormously tall woman with wild gray hair who cackled as she brought the axe down on his head. I imagine he was trying to understand what was happening and that he murmured "why" just before the second blow came. I imagine he remembered a lake long ago and a girl he saw there and that he heard some old music before he had the briefest sense of pain and black took over forever.

If you want a good detective on the case, at least an experienced detective, you're lucky I'm here. A crime like that is virtually unheard of in Plains, or anywhere else, for that matter. Sanders County, Montana, just doesn't get many murders. Probably because Sanders County doesn't have all that many people.

I spent seventeen years on the Seattle police force, the last ten of them as a detective, mostly in homicide. I said, if you want an experienced detective, you're lucky I'm here.

But if you want a tough cop, you've come to the wrong place. My name is Al Barnes, and for years on the Seattle police force I was known as Mush Heart Barnes. I may be the softest cop you've ever seen. When I was a rookie, they first put me on traffic detail, chasing speeders. In one month, I turned in fewer arrests than anyone in the modern history of the force. I set a new record for not giving speeding tickets. My boss, a sergeant named O'Brien, ate my ass out twice, but still I couldn't help myself. I fell for every sob story I heard.

Finally, they took me off traffic and gave me a sort of beat. I cruised around with a partner in a patrol car, hoping always to find things in order. One day we chased and caught some bank robbers. I felt so sorry for the one I held at gunpoint, I felt like letting him go. It struck me at the time that, after all, it was only a system that was out anything, not some individual.

The fact that I'd studied for three years at the University of Washington, majoring in creative writing, of all things, didn't help me when it came to ragtime with my colleagues. I bore their jibes fairly well and went on in my spare time trying to be a poet. The only reason I became a cop was it was the only job I could find at the time, and I was desperate.

Finally, fed up with my weakness, they gave me a job lecturing to grammar school and high school students on the value of the police force to the community. I did OK in public relations work, but a big shake-up in the administration and a new chief who wanted his cops well-rounded found me again in a patrol car.

This time I lucked out and helped solve a series of murders that took place in the Broadway district where we patrolled, my partner and I. I made it into homicide as a beginning detective as a result. And finally, I found something I could do. I was pretty good. For one thing, I don't like murder, and I don't like it even more than most people don't like it. To solve a murder, I could find some toughness in me I could never find with most other crimes.

And I found I had a special gift. I don't know where it came from. People tell me things, and I don't know why. For some reason, people trust me. I must look sympathetic and understanding. It's a handy gift to have when you're investigating a murder. Because most murders are solved by information given to the detective by witnesses, or relatives of either the victim or the killer, or friends of either the victim or the killer—just tips. Most murders are solved because someone tells the detective who did it, in one way or another.

Once a woman told me her husband couldn't have sex without first eating cashew nuts. She said she'd never told anyone that before. Another time a high school teacher told me he had been a homosexual years before that was acceptable. Not only could it have cost him his job, it actually made him a suspect in the murder case I was investigating. My favorite example is the black guy who admitted he'd gotten away with a string of drugstore holdups twenty years before in Dayton, Ohio. I didn't bother to report it. He was living a good life now, had four children, and the information had nothing to do with the murder under investigation. But I asked him why he had told me, and he said, "I don't know, man. You just got the face."

Anyway, as long as the new chief remained, I got shifted around. Narcotics: no arrests in two months. Burglary: three arrests in six weeks. Robbery: one arrest in nine months. So it was back to homicide where I already had a good record. And before I could get shifted again, another shake-up and a new chief and a new policy. I stayed in homicide.

One day I arrested a nice little old man we wanted for questioning. He asked me not to handcuff him, please. His circulation was poor and the cuffs might cut it off entirely, he said. So, true to my nickname, Mush Heart, I told him OK. He asked if he could use the bathroom before we left, and I told him sure. I'd frisked him and knew he wasn't armed. But he was armed when he came out of the bathroom, and he shot me three times.

I just barely made it to the hospital in time. Someone had heard the shots and called the police. They discovered me on the floor amid a lot of my blood. I was in the hospital for seven months; then I took the medical discharge they offered. I was in fairly good shape, but I thought I'd had it with police work. Seattle had gotten bigger and bigger during my seventeen years as a cop, and the work was getting bigger, too. More people, more crime. I got tired of the city, almost as much as the police work there.

But I was forty, and I couldn't do anything else. I had given up trying to be a poet long ago. One cop I liked very much, a big guy named John Mrvich (you had to put a 'u' between the 'M' and 'r' to say it right) had also been interested in writing, and he had kept at it. But years before, he had moved to Portland, something to do with his wife's family, and so my best buddy was gone. Even though my record was good and I had the respect of my colleagues now and was seldom called Mush Heart anymore, staying on didn't appeal to me.

I used the insurance settlement and my old car to buy a new car, and I set out to find some peace and quiet. I'd never gotten married and so at forty was free and feeling adventurous. The pension wasn't really enough to live on, and I needed to do something. I loved Plains, Montana, the first time I saw it.

JAMES CRUMLEY

I did not have a sheltered childhood, but when I met James Crumley (1939–2008), at a party at Limelight in New York when I was in my twenties, I was . . . impressed? Appalled? Amused? He'd driven straight through from Montana, and he was roaring, but roaring in a courtly manner. Later, in Montana, Stacy, Kevin, Steve, and I came to his fifth wedding, to the demure Martha Elizabeth, and they came down from Missoula to Livingston fairly often. One of those times, I remember cleaning up our kitchen at one a.m. after a truly messy dinner party, in all ways, with only Jim as company. He would have flunked multiple types of blood tests, but he talked beautifully, that night, about *Moby Dick*, Gabriel García Márquez, and Raymond Chandler. By the time I went to bed I was in a fine mood.

Jim Crumley grew up poor in South Texas, served in the Philippines during Vietnam, and got an MFA from the Iowa Writers' Workshop in 1966. His thesis became *One to Count Cadence* (1969). Crumley held visiting professorships at a number of universities throughout the seventies (including Colorado State, Reed, and Carnegie Mellon), but when Richard Hugo, then head of the creative writing program at the University of Montana, suggested he read Raymond Chandler, he found his calling. Crumley's novels included *The Wrong Case*, *Dancing Bear*, *The Mexican Tree Duck*, and of course *The Last Good Kiss*, one of the best crime novels of all time (with one of the best titles).

He had another unfinished novel he wanted us to publish; he probably had many unfinished novels.

The Way of the Road

from *The Muddy Fork & Other Things: Short Fiction and Nonfiction*, 1991

by James Crumley

BACK IN THE good old days—or at least our most recent version, the late sixties and the early seventies—every man and boy I knew had a hitchhiking hippie-chick story. You couldn't go into a bar anywhere in the West without hearing half a dozen. Everybody had one—white-shoed insurance salesmen, college professors and lightweight marijuana dealers—everybody, that is, but me. For a time there, it seemed as if I were the only man in the West of an acceptable age who'd never been seduced by random sex, roadsides and great drugs.

But it happens, and it happens like this: you're sitting in your favorite afternoon bar, propped on your favorite bar stool—the one at the end so you can watch the long-legged lady bartender for whom you've conceived a long-term, aimless lust—when she suddenly turns to you and says, "You got a car?" You nod a casual agreement, cool and easy, like a man whose 450 SL is tethered just outside the door. "Does it run?" she asks, having seen such casual nodding before. You reckon it does, and she drops her bar towel to the duckboards, dumps her tip glass into her purse and says, "Well, bud, let's see some highway. I'm so bored with this job I could scream."

The next thing you know, you're in the parking lot of the Outlaw Inn in Kalispell, Montana, watching two rich old drunks argue about workmanship, an argument that has been drifting on for several hours, one old man holding out his Cadillac Sedan de Ville as the epitome of the lost art of craftsmanship and the other opting for his Beretta over and under 12-gauge shotgun. As if to prove his point, the old man with the shotgun fires a round of birdshot through the door of the Cadillac. "Goddamn piece of tin," he mutters as the other old boy rubs his thumb around the splintered metal of the hole in his door, wondering if his insurance will cover gunfire. He reaches under the seat for a quart of Wild Turkey, offers it around, then invites all of us down to his lake house for a three A.M. breakfast. Beside you, the long-legged lady whistles softly, impressed, and squeezes your hand as if you've somehow been responsible for this romantic display.

Come daybreak, you're sitting on the end of a dock watching the sunrise over Flathead Lake. On the western shore, the hills turn golden, the brown grass of late summer glowing between the dark blue horizon and the cold black water. Behind you, the lady bartender argues with the old boys, trying to see how far they will raise the ante just to see her naked. One of the old boys keeps repeating, "Looky but no touchy, looky but no touchy," as he hops from foot to foot like a little boy losing an argument with his bladder. You cannot stop grinning. You know damn well you're drunk, the highway miles buzzing like amphetamines in your head, but lordgodalmighty you feel good for reasons you don't even care to examine. It's an illusion, right; but it's your movie.

Then the lady bartender strides down the dock, her clothes in one hand and a wad of bills in the other, and she drops both in your lap, dives into the icy water and stays under for a long minute. When she surfaces at your feet, she smiles and says, "I want to see sundown in some other goddamned place." And you're back on the road again.

Thus does reality become road myth.

Anybody who has ever spent any time on aimless trips through the mountain West knows that the illusion is of freedom, that lovely freedom of the cowboy, the saddle tramp, the gunfighter, any of those lanky heroes of our movie-screen youths. Somewhere out there great horses wait to be tamed but not broken, fast-gun bullies wait to be vanquished and maybe, if the timing is right, Mona Freeman even waits to be kissed tenderly, just once, before we ride off into a Hollywood sunset.

Of course, we know it isn't like that at all. Mostly the road is drunks and strangers, conversations you didn't mean to have and the loneliness of lying, unable to sleep, in a strange bed in a cheap motel while just beyond the drywall a couple shouts and screams their lonesome way into bed.

But when you're locked in your car, nothing but miles and miles of mountains and miles of straight road before you, you can't help but believe you're a free and better man once again. Whatever ex-wives, lost children and bad debts await you at home, you can put them behind you and that ribbon of highway in front, streaming into your face like a concrete wind.

At least it's always been that way for me.

During the years since I first moved west, I've spent a great deal of road time with a pair of brothers whom, for reasons of decency, I'll call the Buffalo Brothers. They're good road companions, good enough drivers, drunk or sober; willing to spend their money, and large enough to keep us out of trouble in most bars. We've managed to spend lots of lost days on the road, drifting down those winding mountain highways, our teenaged illusions fairly intact well into our forties, starry-eyed and slightly discontent.

One time we were dipping our toes into the Inner Circle (a route of bars north of Missoula, Montana) just to see if we wanted to run for a while, sitting in a bar in Seeley Lake, playing pool with a big kid who worked as a sawyer, a really big kid. We could tell because he had neglected to wear either shoes or a shirt, despite a large sign outside warning against such disgusting behavior. What the hell, it was his home bar—even his home pool table, he thought, until the three of us had beaten him several times running. We had drinks backed up from the bets, and it was becoming clear that the kid wouldn't let us leave without an argument. We discussed losing while he was in the john, but when he came out, he stalked down the bar grabbing everybody's beer cans, full and empty, squeezing them as if they were paper flowers. Occasionally, the beer foam shot all the way to the ceiling, and we squirmed uneasily in our seats. It wasn't our home bar, not by a long shot. But the bartender waved at the big kid as if he were a child, then came around the bar, saying, "Okay boys—that's it."

He picked up two dollies, strode over and set them down near the pool table. He lifted first one end of the pool table, then the other, onto the dollies, then pushed the table toward the far wall where he removed a sheet of plywood and shoved the table into a large niche. Then he came back, replaced the destroyed beers, sat the big kid down on a stool, came over and poured our drinks into large paper cups—"to go."

Nobody said a word. It was one o'clock on a Tuesday afternoon. The Buffalo

Brothers and I hit the road for home, taking the affair as a bad omen, the illusion of survival without pain, or slow-to-heal black eyes, no longer one we held to at all.

Still, for me, driving around beats everything I know. For instance, it took me four tries to understand that I liked driving to ski slopes far better than I liked falling down them with snow packed into my shorts. Once at Eldora, Colorado, the ski patrol sent up a guy to help this buddy of mine and me off the mountain, trying to teach us something simple, like turning, but then he threw up his poles in despair and led us as we bombed down the slope.

I took that as an omen, too. Nothing at ski slopes appeals to me. You have to climb on or into pieces of machinery, then be carried off the ground, fall down a lot, get so cold that not even a sauna bakes it out of your bones and drink with a bunch of pretentious people wearing funny clothes. Skiing is not my idea of recreation.

And I'm not all that crazy about backpacking. I've done it just three times in the past fifteen years, and every trip was fraught with disasters both major and minor. If you go alone, you get lonesome. If you go with other people, you often discover just who your friends aren't. The fishing is never as good as it's supposed to be; the rain is always wetter inside a tent on a mountain than anyplace else. And I've never been able to pack enough whiskey to make it bearable.

Hunting used to be fun, admittedly; but as I've gotten older it seems too much like work, and I'm a bit ashamed of the thrill I get when I kill a deer or an elk. So I've given up killing them and taken to trading goods or services for my meat. I'd much rather stay in camp all day cooking and washing dishes so that everybody else will feel guilty and give me a share of the meat.

I never cared much for trout fishing, either, since I was raised in southern Texas using trotlines, crank telephones and quarter sticks of dynamite. So I often fail to see the beauty of standing butt-deep in an avalanche of cold water while a barbed hook snaps past my ear. This may go back to one afternoon when I was sitting in the Golden Ram in Fort Collins, Colorado, and a friend of mine came in after a windy day of fly-fishing on the Cache La Poudre. He sat down beside me and ordered a double Scotch straight with a double on the rocks as a chase. His bald head was resplendent: two

Renegades and a Royal Coachman were lodged securely in the right side of his scalp. "Don't say a word," he muttered. "Don't say a goddamn word." Quite enough said about the joys of fly-fishing.

I might not use the mountains for the sort of serious recreation that some people engage in, but I like to drive through them. If I'm away from them very long I get as homesick as a bird dog kenneled for six weeks during quail season. I guess I still have a flatlander's awe at the simple size of these mountains. I like to look at them the same way some people like to look at the sea. I like to look at them even from the parking lot of the Eastgate Liquor Store and Lounge in Missoula, where the view includes railroad tracks, an interstate and a battery of gasoline storage tanks.

I leave but always come back to these lovely, perfectly useless mountains, these dingy, polluted western towns where the wages are low and the prices are high and the living is often hard. Judging by the growth rates of western towns, though, I'm not the only person in the country who comes to the West with the illusion of freedom. Not by a long shot.

Art & Miscellany

THIS ANTHOLOGY can't do justice to the press's volumes of art and photography, or to the paintings on its covers. The collection *Russell Chatham* first came out with Winn Books in 1984, and Clark City reprinted it in 1987. The reproductions are superb, and the writing is priceless (see Tom McGuane's piece on page 3). *The Missouri Headwaters*, showing Russell's stunning print work—twelve 34-by-45-inch lithographs, each named for a month—was a successful attempt to break into that market, and *One Hundred Paintings* was a beautiful but more expensive piece of advertising, and not an easy thing to pull off.

Russell, having grown up with them, was devoted to the Wolo books and intent on bringing them to a new generation.

I hope you will look up the beautiful work of Stephen Collector and Diana Guest, and I wish I could do more to celebrate Peter Stackpole. Images from their books can be found in the insert section.

* * *

STEPHEN COLLECTOR

Law of the Range was one of Russell's passion projects, an ode to the West, and its fifty portraits of brand inspectors resonate from the beautifully printed pages. Stephen Collector's (1951–) images have appeared in countless magazines and newspapers, including *The New York Times*, *Esquire*, *Outside*, and *Men's Journal*, and he is still doing wonderful work out of Boulder, Colorado.

What You See Is What You Got

introduction by Annick Smith

Law of the Range: Portraits of Old-Time Brand Inspectors, 1991, by Stephen Collector

THE OLD MEN SQUINT into the light with small hard eyes. Their faces are ridged as home-milled cross-cut pine. The old men have dressed up in new jeans fastened with silver rodeo buckles. The buckles are badges earned long ago when they rode broncs or roped in dusty arenas from Colorado to the Canadian border. The old men do not smile. We know they have scraped cowshit off their polished go-to-town boots.

In the background are faraway mountains—the Tetons, the Big Horns, the Rockies—or a sweep of grass, or wheat, or the mud-brown South Platte, high with spring runoff, glinting beyond the sagebrush. We imagine hoot owls, the dissonant cries of red-winged blackbirds in the tules.

There are no women anywhere. Sometimes there is a spotted horse and a dog. One old dude sits in a Butte café. Another straddles a bar stool. A few of the softer, bespectacled sort have chosen to be pictured in an office. Several, too stove-up to wield the most cherished tool of their trade, seem to caress coiled ropes with arthritic hands. Painted on walls, on old bar siding are hieroglyphics—the beloved brands.

Their names are Orlin Corn, Bill Apple, Lyman Edgar, Elston Spatz, turn-of-the-century Anglo, German, Scandinavian names you find in obituaries from newspapers in every western hamlet. In such names we recognize a dominant strain in the white man's settlement of the plains. These are the grandfathers and bachelors who die unnoticed in old people's homes.

PETER STACKPOLE

As one of the four original *Life* photographers (with Margaret Bourke-White, Alfred Eisenstaedt, and Thomas McAvoy), Peter Stackpole (1913–1997), son of the great sculptor Ralph Stackpole, captured decades of Hollywood at play and at work: Elizabeth Taylor on her bike, heading home from high school; Errol Flynn on his sailboat with his beloved dog; Orson Welles working on a script while Rita Hayworth sunbathes below by the pool.

Russell desperately wanted to bring Peter back into the limelight. His stunning non-Hollywood work included war photography, *The Bridge Builders* (a portfolio for *Vanity Fair* of the construction of the San Francisco Bay Bridge), and *Smokejumpers, '49*.

The timing of this book was both lucky and tragic: While it was in production, Peter lost everything in the 1991 Oakland fire, including virtually all the negatives for these photos.

Peter Stackpole: Life in Hollywood, 1936–1952

from the introduction by Peter Stackpole, 1992

THE PLACE TO LIVE was near the beach in Santa Monica Canyon. I would drive Sunset Boulevard all the way to the office. Our first house was a small white hillside shack, but the second rental was a virtual mansion—three stories, surrounded by sycamore trees, on Mesa Road, where our neighbors included Edward and Brett Weston . . . . The studio beat introduced me to the big publicity factories. Nothing I'd encountered in New York prepared me for the VIP treatment I received. Call a studio, and the operator called you honey. Drop by, and lunch was free. Need to be somewhere, and they'd send a limousine. Express interest in a star and an appointment was made. Around Christmas, baskets of liquor, fruit, candy and wine arrived, again by limousine. The studios would send tickets to all the premieres and previews, some of which we covered for the sake of the Klieg-lighted spectacle.

Such was the power of *Life* in those days, but I remained a determined voyeur, not a fan.

DIANA GUEST

Diana Guest (1909–1994), whose mother was an heir to the Phipps fortune and whose father was Winston Churchill's first cousin, didn't let wealth blinker the scope of her interests. She learned to fly and spent time with the Blixen–Finch-Hatton crowd in Kenya, she raised racehorses, and during the last half of her life she created elemental, subtle, beautiful sculptures out of bronze and alabaster, onyx and marble and soapstone, which she exhibited in Paris, New York, Zurich, Palm Beach, and London. Today they can be found in private and museum collections around the world, and one small bronze owl flies in the corner of my garden.

Introductory Essay

by Jim Harrison

Stonecarver, 1993, by Diana Guest

TWENTY YEARS AGO or so I stopped in France in late October after a longish trip to the Soviet Union. I left Leningrad in a soul-humbling blizzard, the ferocity of which caused our plane to pirouette on the runway, and landed at Bourget, where I immediately kissed the ground on one of those sun-blasted late autumn days that remind us of their own glorious selves. The next morning I drove with Diana Guest's son, and my friend, Guy de la Valdène, out to her five-hundred-year-old home and horse farm in Normandy, entering a world far stranger to me than Leningrad.

It did not occur to me until I left ten days later that I was leaving a heraldic world where an artist's work resonated the deep past with improbable vividness. Diana's sculpted swans, owls, hawks and horses emerged there and belonged to the soul of the landscape (if you do not believe the land has a soul, look at land that has lost it). It was a reality with a distant but direct relationship to the one we know from tapestries, a reality that emerges from bestiaries written when animals held far more significance than as fodder for environmental squabbles, animals that retained a sacred position in our lives in contrast to something we merely use, take advantage of, that cannot be allowed to exist by and for themselves, or are indulged only if their habitat is not useful to us. One loved them, ate them, chased them, created myths from them—they were not ideas but fellow creatures who shared our joys and dooms.

After so many years I came to know and understand Diana's work more closely, the unmeasurable grace by which she returns the animal its name which had grown meaningless by misuse. Sculpture, like poetry, painting and music, keeps our waning gods alive, restores their youth. Her sculpture is nearly Native American in its simplicity, stopping the world for a moment, as all good art does. Her animals have been given back their "otherness" and are no longer glyphs for our ideas about them. In her work she reaches into this "otherness" and brings it back to us, life forms that we only comprehend in rarest moments, as John Muir did his beloved bears: "Bears are made of the same dust as we and breathe the same winds and drink the same waters, his life not long, not short, knows no beginning, no ending, to him life unstinted, unplanned, is above the accident of time, and his years, markless, boundless, equal eternity."

The Last Catalogue

THE PAGES THAT FOLLOW are a reader we used instead of a traditional catalogue for the last season, Spring 1993, in an attempt to really prove the point: We planned to publish some beautiful books. All of these titles except Peter Matthiessen's ultimately made it to print with other presses, with our typeset and design.

* * *

A Clark City Press Reader

Spring 1993

A Clark City Press Reader
Spring 1993

An excerpt from

Red & Blue Days

Writings on the American West

by Peter Matthiessen

The Sioux believe that at the end of the world the moon will turn red and the sun will turn blue, and the Lakota people will resume their place at the center of existence.

The poorest of the poor—by far—are the Indian people. It is true that in our courts today the Indian has legal status as a citizen, but anyone familiar with Indian life, in cities or on reservations, can testify that justice for Indians is random and arbitrary where it exists at all. For all our talk about suppression of human rights in other countries, and despite a nostalgic sentimentality about the noble Red Man, the prejudice and persecution still continue. American hearts respond with emotion to Indian portraits by George Catlin and Edward Curtis, to such eloquent books as *Black Elk Speaks* and *Bury My Heart at Wounded Knee*, to modern films and television dramas in which the nineteenth-century Indian is portrayed as the tragic victim of Manifest Destiny; we honor his sun dances and thunderbirds in the names of our automobiles and our motels. Our nostalgia comes easily, since those stirring peoples are safely in the past, and the abuse of their proud character, generosity, and fierce honesty—remarked upon by almost all the first Europeans to observe them—can be blamed upon our roughshod frontier forebears. "The tribes who once owned this country" were simply in the way of the white man's progress, and so most of the eastern tribes were removed to Indian Territory (now Oklahoma), and the western tribes mostly banished or confined to arid wastes that no decent white man would want. By a great historical irony, many of these lands were situated on the dry crust of the Grants Mineral Belt, which extends from the lands of the Dene people in Saskatchewan to those of their close relatives, the Dine, or "Navajo," in New Mexico and Arizona, and contains North America's greatest energy resources. More than half of the continent's uranium and much of its petroleum and coal lie beneath Indian land, and so the Indians are in the way again.

After four hundred years of betrayals and excuses, Indians recognize the new fashion in racism, which is to pretend that the real Indians are all gone. We have no wish to be confronted by these "half-breeds" of today, gone slack after a century of enforced dependence, poverty, bad food, alcohol, and despair, because to the degree that these people can be ignored, the shame of our nation can be ignored as well. Leonard Peltier's experience reflects more than most of us wish to know about the realities of Indian existence in America; our magazines turn away from articles about the Indians of today, and most studies of Indian history and culture avoid mention of the twentieth century. But the Indians are still among us—"We are your shadows," one man says— and the qualities they were known for in their days of glory still persist among many of these quiet people, of mixed ancestry as well as full-blood, who still abide in the echo of the Old Way.

Doug Peacock describes his first experience with grizzlies in that late summer of 1968 in Yellowstone. He was camped by a hot spring some distance from the road when, hearing strange snufflings, he peered out of his tent and saw a grizzly sow with two cubs at the wood edge fifty yards away. Though the bears paid him no attention, he climbed a lodgepole pine in terror. Since that day he has spent two decades studying grizzly behavior, and most grizzly biologists would grant that this untrained loner has had more experience with wild grizzlies—bears that have never been exposed to human company—than anyone alive.

Years ago, Peacock was seriously threatened by a large male grizzly that prowled around his tent all night despite his hasty bonfires, and he says he never sleeps much in bear country. Most fatal encounters in recent years have occurred at night, when a predatory bear drags a human denizen out of a sleeping bag. It was two completely separate fatalities on the same stormy night in August 1967 here in Glacier—both young women, neither in a tent—that inspired the Park Service to close its dumps. Since then, says Doug Peacock, six more humans have been killed by bears in Glacier and three in Yellowstone; four of these victims were dragged out of tents or bags.

"When I'm alone," Peacock admits, "I keep twigs and paper handy for a bonfire, I lie in the very middle of the tent, and I don't sleep much." Since this night is too wet for bonfires, and since both occupants must lie pressed to the tent walls, we make do with a discussion of our bear deterrent. "I don't come in here armed," Peacock sighs, "so I guess it's nice to have *something* to fall back on. Lets you sleep a little." But in inexperienced hands, he adds, the canister would probably be more dangerous than effective, bolstering false confidence when what is needed is alertness and experience with bear behavior. Pepper in the snout or eye at the wrong moment might provoke a curious grizzly that might otherwise have gone its way in peace. "Sooner or later," he says, "someone will get hurt or killed using one of these, and it won't be the bear."

In the late sixties, preferring the dull onus of overgrazed range to headlines about cruel slaughter of wild animals, Yellowstone Park began to "monitor" rather than manage the resurgent herds of elk and bison. It also continued to suppress all fire, although ecologists expressed alarm about the buildup of dead fuel wood in the forests. In 1972, responding to the urging of conservation organizations, Yellowstone initiated a police of "natural burn," which permitted wild fires started by lightning to burn themselves out except where they threatened the works of man. It resisted the idea of "prescribed burning," in which certain areas would be burned under controlled circumstances—in short, land management, which was anathema to the park philosophy of every organism (except the tourist) for itself. In recent years, the park's shamefully inadequate scientific research, according to one indefatigable critic—Alston Chase, author of *Playing God in Yellowstone*—has amounted to less than 2 percent of a budget dedicated to visitor comfort and protection.

"Natural burn" met its first real test in the dry year of 1979, when a number of lightning fires went along unmolested. The next year, an infestation of the pine-bark beetle added many more trees to the buildup of storm blow-down and dry fuel. In the early 1980's came a drought of seven years that intensified sharply after 1985. Unusually wet springs and summers were unable to offset thin snow packs, which lowered water levels and dried out the land. Then came a record drought year, 1988, when a meager snow pack and a wet spring followed the pattern, but dry, hot, windy summer days did not. The summer of 1988 had the lowest rainfall recorded in the park since 1876, the dusty year of Custer's death on the Little Bighorn. Drought and wind together brought about the million-acre accident that, according to park critics, had been waiting to happen for a hundred years.

On June 23, a lightning fire started at Shoshone Lake, in the southwest, and on June 25 what became the Fan fire was reported in the northwest corner of the park. In the next weeks, six other smoke plumes rose from the dark conifers to the blue sky. Because all but two (the North Fork and Hellroaring) were lightning fires, all but two were allowed to burn. Not until after mid-July, when the Shoshone fire and the Fan were already large, and the Clover fire (which had joined the Mist in the northeast) was a good deal larger, did park officials attack the Shoshone, mostly because it had come too close to the park community of Grant Village. People fearing a loss of tourist business were already saying that after three years of low rainfall, the park should have recognized the drought and acted earlier. On July 21, responding to howls of catastrophe from the public and its election-year politicians, park officials suspended "natural burn" indefinitely, in favor of the greatest firefighting effort in United States history . . .

On the mountain prairie by Alum Creek was a herd of several hundred bison, and beyond the creek, along the northwest side of Hayden Valley, the black wall of the North Fork fire. Accidently started by a woodcutter in Idaho's Targhee Forest on July 22, 1988, it went on to become the largest of the Yellowstone fires and the only one not yet "contained"—surrounded by fire lines—by Oct. 19, the day of my arrival. On the west side of the road, to Canyon Village and beyond, most trees still standing were black limbless spires, with burned-out logs on bare black earth. A pervasive stench of rain-soaked ash was disagreeably sweet and harsh at the same time.

Here in this scene of desolation, my assumption that the National Park Service must be at fault began to undergo a cautious change. I saw no sign of contented elk chomping new green shoots in the blackened forest, as suggested by recent news releases, but this stark scene seemed far less dreadful than press accounts of 200-foot-high flames, charred moonscapes and fleeing citizens had me prepared for. It looked as if high winds had caused the flames to rush here and there in finger patterns, leaving countless patches of green forest within the outer perimeters of each fire. Even in places of most awesome burn, one was never out of sight of live green trees, which would very soon reseed these blackened areas.

Instead of gloom at the seeming "loss," the vast charred prospect, there came instead a heady sense of the earth opening outward, of mountain light and imminent regeneration, which made me recall how oppressive I once found the south part of the park, with its monotone enclosing stands of lodgepole pine. Far from being stunned by the destruction, I felt an exhilaration and relief, as if Yellowstone Park, for the first time in a century, had gotten a deep breath of fresh air.

☾ ☾ ☾

. . . I walked back from the *boca* on the ocean shore, inspecting the myriad seashells from the Pacific . . . Flocks of shorebirds—plovers and sandpipers of several species—stood one-legged on the points in a hard wind, and in the distance a dead whale lay in the surf, attended by gulls and a pair of turkey vultures (a century ago, those vultures might have been condors). Swollen a pink-purple, the whale was still intact, its flipper jutting into the Pacific sky as rusty and barnacled as an old rudder. The coyotes would come to gnaw at it at night, and the crabs, copepods, and snails were already mining the vast trove of matter from beneath.

The weather is unsettled, no two days alike. Sun, rain, and wind. We cross over to the mainland shore and cast into the mangroves for grunt and snapper.

Every supper we have fine fresh fish, for the fish here are still plentiful and unsophisticated, especially the cabrilla, a delicious rock bass, and even the children in the camp are expert fishermen.

My small tent sits between greened knolls on a dune of fine light pale sand above the channel. The sand is sprinkled with white shell of perished land snails, ten to the square foot, often many more, although there is no sign of live snails in the sparse dune cover. At the foot of the dune, along the water, a gifted crab or copepod creates an extraordinary spray of wet sand in its tidal excavations, its hole a mere pinpoint at the flower's base. From my tent each morning I can hear and watch the puff and blow of whales and dolphins; a young sea lion, as if anxious to be petted, haunts our shore.

On the last afternoon, in cool wind and shifting light, I walk north over the dunes, lost in so much solitude and silence. Small flocks of curlews whistle over the wheat-colored sand, as if preparing for the long flight north in a few weeks' time. Brant geese and white pelicans travel up and down the channel, sometimes a hundred brant in a single flock, or seventy or more of the rare pelicans. On the far shore, against the mangroves and the desert, stands a single egret, white as bone.

When the boat comes for us on the last morning, I ask the fisherman the name of our island. "*No se,*" he says, looking confused. "*No hay nombre.*" All this empty place, he tells us, waving his arms, is Magdalena.

Among Indians, the concept of an art separate from nature, of which life is part, is as unnatural as the idea of a life separated from religion. Rock painting, tent symbols, body paint, sand paintings, blankets, moccasins, belts, baskets, even jewelry, had signs that transmitted a teaching, and the most sacred signs were withheld from objects manufactured for the white man; for in a life that is not separate from religious experience, such objects may be dangerous, containing the power of a world in which there are no accidents. This power is not to be corrupted. To weave a basket is to reenact the process of creation, and the finished basket is the image of the universe. Only recently, in imitation of the white man, have Indians signed their work; they would approve of Georgia O'Keeffe, who when asked, "Why don't you sign your work?" responded, "Why don't you sign your face?"

Since an art (or an artist) as something apart from daily existence is not recognized, "the basis for aesthetic judgment is mystical"; that is, it is rich or poor in quality according to the amount of power it can bring about. The words of songs were less important than the state of mind evoked, since these elevated states were protective and curative; in other words, these poem/songs were valued as much for the reaction in oneself as for the effect on others. All songs had a certain power, returning the singer to harmony with the life force, the Great Mystery, that permeates all of creation.

As a Blackfoot says: "I meditated often upon the powers in the air, water and earth. They are the great mysteries. Everything is done by them . . . I spent hours on the hilltop and near the waters, meditating and watching the birds, animals and heavens."

PETER MATTHIESSEN had already begun his writing career by the time he graduated from Yale University in 1950. As a naturalist-explorer, he has been a member of expeditions to remote regions of all five continents and he has worked as a commercial fisherman and captain of a charter boat. Mr. Matthiessen is the author of over twenty books including *The Snow Leopard* (winner of the National Book Award), *The Tree Where Man Was Born* and *At Play in the Fields of the Lord* (both nominated for the National Book Award). His fiction includes the novels *Killing Mister Watson, Far Tortuga,* and *Race Rock* and the collection *On the River Styx and Other Stories.* His works of nonfiction include *The Cloud Forest* and *Under the Mountain Wall* (which together received an Award of Merit from the National Institute of Arts and Letters), *Nine-Headed Dragon River, Men's Lives, African Silences,* and *Baikal: Sacred Sea of Siberia.* He is currently working on a companion novel to *Killing Mister Watson.*

Sworn Before Cranes

by Merrill Gilfillan

At first glance, nothing in the valley appears animate, unless you count the few snowflakes hedging from a glaring white sky as animate, or the ice-edged low-water creeks knifing their crooked ways. Even the frozen dirt roads, snow-white against the pale grasslands, show no tracks or signs of passage.

But when the eye adjusts it sees at last a thin trail of smoke from a wooden house hidden in streamside trees. Then a dark northern hawk shakes itself on a cottonwood limb and from a solitary trailer guyed to a distant knoll a hunched old woman in a black overcoat and calico babushka walks slowly to the hand pump in her yard. That iron and that water will be cold today.

Along the worn highway moves a car from the south. A large, shining American car. Inside it sit two young men absentmindedly listening to the radio. By their cropped hair and antennaless look and skinny black ties, they are Mormons, in search of prey. A man standing by that highway would hear the car coming for a long way, and then hear it going for a long, long way.

At the end of one of the frozen-rut roads, in a home beside a woody trickle of a stream, coffee is boiling for the Keeps Guns. It is a home with all the necessities and arm's reach of a good camp; a smart, durable camp with a multigeneration feel to it.

Two boys are mending a homemade basketball goal near the house. The summer shade-arbor's pinebough roof is sere red and drooping. The outhouse is a patchwork of mixed planks and sheet metal, standing at the edge of the creek's box elders. Near the main house stand an empty eighty-year-old log home, a deer butchering gantry, and a couple of sheds, tipi poles leaning against one of them. Then, the good deep well, engineless cars rilled with rough overflow storage, a brown horse and a colt, laundry frozen on the line, a big pile of firewood.

The father of the family is drinking coffee, idly watching the boys hammer down a flap in the backboard. They work with gloves on from the hood of a car. Dogs loiter about the yard. A grandmother sits near the warm stove. A grandchild crawls in the kitchen, rolling an onion along as it goes. The mother sits at the table packing gifts to be mailed to their other boy in prison over in the Falls. She fits in candy and cigarettes and a braid of sweet grass and ties it up good and tight.

It will be Christmas in four or five days and they are meatless, but they don't dwell on it. They know it but don't dwell on it, because they know in the same way that things will set up in their own good time, or not set up, which is a setup just as well.

One night summer before last, up in the Montana Blackfeet country, two boys were driving south on the Choteau highway. They were drinking and getting drunk. The boy driving was a Blackfeet boy, the other was a white boy from Arkansas. They got into an argument over something, probably money, and the white boy reached up and turned on the dome light and pulled out a pistol and shot the Blackfeet boy as he was driving down the road. Shot him dead and grabbed the wheel and pulled off the highway and dumped the body out into the ditch, took his money and cigarettes and Tony Lama boots and drove on. Twenty minutes later a patrol car stopped him for speeding. It was a woman cop. The boy shot her too when she walked up to the car window. At the trial all his family and his girlfriend were up from Arkansas, sitting there stiffly in the stands. They were there to support the boy. They ate at the same hamburger place every night. The girlfriend was arrested for trying to slip the boy a knife in jail.

The same week, down in Miles City, some young Cheyennes were drinking in a bar, getting drunk. These were people who had moved up to Miles to live for a while. They were talking to a white boy, a half-silly boy with a gimpy leg. He was drunk too. They all talked loud and laughed loud and watched on the bias to see if the white boy was laughing as loud as themselves. When the place closed up they all decided to go somewhere together. They got in one of the Cheyennes' car and drove out the Baker road, drinking. The Cheyennes started talking Cheyenne. They stopped at a little park ten miles out of town and stopped laughing and began working the white boy for money. They beat him up bad and stabbed him and he died up under the pines on a pocky concrete picnic table. They caught those kids two days later down in Sheridan, Wyoming.

But the deal that the Keeps Gun boy was in on happened over toward Yankton, South Dakota. It happened a few days after the Miles City incident, in one of those ugly little South Dakota towns conceived when a locomotive stopped for water and a handful of Europeans materialized to sell things to one another.

There was a bully in this little town, a white man about forty years old. He could hardly write his name. For twenty years his family had bullied the Sioux people around this town. Stared at them through slitty eyes. Insulted them so they could hear it. Slurped and slapped at the pretty Sioux girls. Beat up men and spit on their boots, and in winter drove by so they splashed slush on Indians walking along the road.

This one man was the worst of the bunch. Everybody knew about him. The police were afraid to cross him. He was a bully of the sort you heard about in the old Indian stories, old old stories of the half-human bully-monsters who killed people for laughs and took all the good meat for themselves. People used to know what to do in those situations.

The Keeps Gun boy was over visiting people in this town. He was over there for two or three weeks. One afternoon the bully was drinking hard. Then he began driving down through the Indian part of town, yelling at people, insulting them, scaring the children off the streets. The Keeps Gun boy was right there, helping his friend work on his pickup truck.

When the bully drove off, the friend said, "Come on," and they got in a car and drove downtown to the police station and asked them to keep the bully out of the Indian housing before things got bad. Then they went back home.

A policeman pulled the bully over downtown and told him on the qt that an Indian had filed a complaint about him and advised him to go home and sleep it off. And then he told the bully which Indian had come to the station.

Just after dark, the Keeps Gun boy and his friend had the truck running and drove downtown to buy some beer. Keeps Gun sat in the truck while the older boy went across the street into the liquor store. When the Sioux boy was coming out of the store, Keeps Gun heard someone yelling and looked around and saw the bully coming out from a parking lot with another white man.

The bully came at the Indian and grabbed him by the arm and knocked the Old Milwaukee to the ground. Then the other white man tried to hold the boy's arms from behind and in a minute the whole thing blew. Two Sioux boys came running down the street with a hoe handle and they were all swinging and kicking. Keeps Gun jumped out and grabbed a length of two-by-four from the truck bed and ran into the fight.

Some of the other men had clubs as well, but a prosecution expert, and then the jury with tight thin lips, said it was the Keeps Gun boy who caught the bully at the base of the skull with his two-by-four and killed him.

It was nothing like the magical acrobatic antibully finesse of a thousand years earlier in this territory, but the monster was dead and stinking there in the parking-lot lights.

So now they had packed him up some cigarettes and sweet grass and sent it to him in prison over in the Falls. It is two days before Christmas. There will be relatives coming from Antelope and Spring Creek. The grandmother and the mother begin thinking a little more about meat. They haul the big sack of potatoes out from the side room and look them over to see that they are all good. They get out the big boxes of dried corn and check to see if mice have gotten to them and set them out on the kitchen counter. They think about the meat but don't mention it aloud.

Late in the day the two boys are sitting at the table in the house. The women are folding laundry and the father is drinking coffee, looking out at the hills. Then the older boy says, "Let's go," and the two of them get up and put on their coats and retrieve a rifle from the corner and say, "We'll be back later," and leave the house.

They drive in the pickup out to the highway and south a mile, where they turn off to pick up another boy. It is just getting dark. The three drive for half an hour, west on a state highway, then north on a minor paved road, a little-traveled, houseless road that rolls and bucks through the anonymous leased grazing lands toward the rough country of the Cuny Table.

It is full dark now and the work is simple and has been done before. On an open, lightless stretch of the highway they see cattle near the fence. They cut the radio and pull over and check both ways on the road for car lights and put the flashlight on a gaping Hereford and shoot it with the .30-30 from the cab. Two of the boys jump out of the truck and over the fence while the third drives off and up the long climb to the table where he will pull off the highway and wait.

The two boys in the field cut the Hereford's throat and roll her on her back. They set the flashlight on the ground and work with large hardware butcher knives honed on a flat file. They work quickly, watching for cars on the highway. When lights come down the hill from the table, they shut off the flashlight and crouch, ready to run. When the car passes they are back at it. *Wheep, wheep,* a knife whipping on the file. They take just the four legs of the cow, severing the shoulder and hip joints with a hatchet. They drag the quarters over to the fence and under the barbed wire.

They wait low in the dark ditch until the driver comes back down the hill and swerves over to the fence side of the road. They haul the four drumsticks up to the berm and heave them into the truck bed and throw a tarp over them and drive away.

On Christmas Day the soup was made and bubbling on the Keeps Gun stove for whoever might want it. It was good old-fashioned soup with dried corn and salt pork and beef in it. There was an inch of day-old snow on the yard where the dogs shivered and wandered from car tire to car tire to sniff the new arrivals: cars and trucks from Spring Creek and Antelope. Magpies sat on the Keeps Gun house watching everything that moved or was about to move.

Inside, the solstitial social heart was beating. The television was on at one end of the room and the radio at the other. The various generations gravitated to their own kind. Children laughed and chased. Three grandmothers sat together in a corner, so old and leaflike and primary that they communicated by the positions of their hands in their quiet laps.

Midafternoon, a Catholic priest stopped by the home with Christmas greetings and a sack of oranges. He was learning to speak Lakota and always told funny stories about his recent linguistic trials and errors. He was a jovial man who wore white sneakers the year round. He sat at the table with mother and father and ate a bowl of the hot soup—*wahanpi, wahanpi,* he practiced as he ate.

The Catholic priest drove off and before long an Episcopal preacher drove in. There was candy for the children. It was remarkably like the Catholic father's visit. The Episcopal was a good-natured man with pink cheeks and pink furry ears. He ate a bowl of the soup and smiled and then the quick receding footsteps—*quack, quack, quack*—on the cold driveway snow just as the day was fading and the dogs were creeping under the porch to their rag beds.

An hour later, the jovial priest was still making his rounds. At the moment he was driving on the dark straightaway past the very pasture where the cow was butchered, driving through the quizzical, caged-bird silence of jovial people alone.

And that night there were those saying that rocks and stones are the oldest things on earth. But there were others who might be saying that that quartered beef lying eyes open in that starry, rumpled Christmas field—that frozen, sleighless, life-biding fuselage—is the oldest thing on earth.

MERRILL GILFILLAN is the author of three books of poetry: *Light Years, To Creature,* and *River through Rivertown;* and a collection of essays, *Magpie Rising: Sketches from the Great Plains,* which was awarded the 1989 PEN / Martha Albrand Award for Nonfiction. He currently lives in Boulder, Colorado.

An excerpt from

The Massacre at Sand Creek

A Narrative by Bruce Cutler

From the Foreword

On November 29, 1864, in the last weeks of the Civil War, volunteer forces under the command of Colonel John Milton Chivington attacked a peaceful camp of Cheyennes located along Sand Creek in the south central part of the Colorado territory. What ensued was genocide, and hundreds of Cheyenne and Arapaho men, women, and children were massacred. John Smith, a well known mountain man who was visiting the camp at the time, had his life spared, but his half-Cheyenne son was killed, and Smith was forced to watch as the body was dragged around the camp behind the horses of Chivington's men.

A force of cavalry seconded from Fort Lyon and under the command of Captain Silas Soule refused to obey Chivington's orders and would not fire on the encampment. The ensuing dispute over Soule's refusal and the actions of Chivington's forces generated several Congressional inquiries, all of which found that Chivington had ordered an unprovoked assault.

Like My Lai and other massacres committed during wartime, the massacre at Sand Creek came at the end of a period of escalating tensions between indigenous peoples and whites who were at war on more than one front. And while news of the massacre was followed by public concern and outcry, none of that served in the end to change the attitudes held by most nineteenth and twentieth century Americans. On the contrary, it served as the beginning of widespread warfare on the plains between white Americans and "Indians." The feelings of indifference, or scorn, or fear that most white Americans had for "Indians" would persist, even after a tidal wave of demand for the rights of subject peoples had swept the continents of the world, and ours along with them, more than a century later. — Bruce Cutler

From Part One

The Wolves of Heaven
Northern Cheyenne Reservation, Montana
August 14, 1911

What really belongs to anybody, except what they have already lived? What has anybody to live for, except what they are not yet living? —Cesare Pavese

They're camped in short-grass country, but it isn't theirs.
In a place that they've been given, if given is what
you can't say "no" to.
A place that they would ride through
to get to another place, if the troops would let them.
To a place where sky and earth connect, where the spirit
world can bless and guide the living. Where all
can know the dead when living, and the living when they're dead.
In peace.

*

Instead, they dig. The man and woman take
turns, under a stone-colored sky. Not a tree,
not a thing that moves except for the glint
of the mattock, rising, falling.
There's a bundle at their feet.
It's wrapped in grasses and a bolt of flannel, tied
with thongs. It has come to her from Oklahoma
from a cousin of a cousin who came on the thing it holds.
In a white man's store of hand-me-downs. The cousin
had known at once, wedged as it was in a corner
in back of shoes and purses where it lived on, forgotten.
It was tanned and supple and bordered with a casing
stitched in red, with a French silk drawstring run
inside to close it. No need for a second look,
she'd known.
How could the white man know? What he felt
he let pass through his heart. It left him without memory,
in ignorance that spared him from the gall of shame.

*

She thinks: you can ask of Owl "Who are the most
on earth, the living or the dead?" and Owl will say
"The dead!" And there you are, truth is told
on you, say as you will "Since when is it
success for anyone to die?"
For saying that
you betray a heart that doubts the wonder of this world.
This place where fear should never light its fire.
This place of transformations. Deathlessness. Miracle.

*

So she asks nothing. This thing that is now a bauble
has passed from hand to hand, relative to relative,
has made its way as a stray dog would across
the plains, until it found her. Cradled by hands,
by palms, by fingers, it took on life, came out
of its past like a ghost, branded with the name of the man
who once had worked it into shape, "Squiers, S. Crk.,
1864."
          And it was truly a child
of its maker. So cunning, so aweless it could stay on a shelf
or in back of a drawer for years unless you took it
carefully in hand, felt its surface, traced
its contours down to the hard unyielding areole
and nipple at the bottom. Then you would have known.

The cousins, they had known. And now the woman
has it, this piece, this bit of pelt that never
was the pouch it posed as, that never served
a purpose other than to fit a message to your hand,
terrible phylactery of the faith that holds an Indian
less than a living soul.
                    Tit-bag, soldiers
called it. It has come along with wizened fingers,
scalplocks, scrotums stretched into humidors,
the file of body parts that slipped away
in pockets, kit-bags, trunks, leaving the plains
for courthouse squares, banquet halls, museums.

And then into the long dark night of dresser drawers,
attic trunks. Waiting. Continuing to be.
Biding the time until their time would come again.

Today, she's vowed she'll give it burial. She,
the woman, Ekomina, granddaughter of Crow Woman that died
in the white man's trap at Sandy Creek. She,
at work with her husband, Frank Little Wolf. The two of them,
pledgers for the Massaum. But first they must dig a narrow
house for the thousandth part of one of them, their people,
Tsistsistas.

From Part Three

The Attack
November 29, 1864

If men would learn from history, what lessons it might teach us! But passion and party blind our eyes, and the light which experience gives is a lantern on the stern which shines only on the waves behind us! — S. T. Coleridge

Soule is in command of Company D,
Colorado First. He keeps them well apart
from the Colonel's troops, if troops are what you call them—
Central City miners, flooded out
last summer, in for a hundred days of pay
then back to the diggings. Only a very few
with stomachs for a real campaign, and now with this cold
sick to death of soldiering. The kind of troops
no one can command, that early in this war to save
the Union proved the depths of their Dutch courage.
Ragtag volunteers that come sweeping down on Regulars
compelling them to do the dirty work

for Colonel Lunatic, for Chiv, as they call him,
whose evening entertainment starts when the cook
gets mad at someone, throws a burning brand
streaming like a comet, and soon the air is full
of brands, it's Farragut at New Orleans,
the night becomes a blaze of meteors
and shooting stars, and in the end there is no supper,

not even coffee, the volunteers get whooping
drunk while their Colonel sits indoors, dressing
down the officers. This former circuit rider,
this Mason Methodist, size fourteen boots,
says he's come to bring them to a rendezvous. An apocalypse.

Dawn. Steel-gray as birdshot. They're riding on a sand hill
with the creek curving across the line of march
below. Only a gleam of water there,
cottonwoods and willows along the banks.
Clumps of lodges thrown down like pine cones catch
the sun's first rays. He counts a hundred fifteen,
eight Arapaho, the rest Cheyenne. Soule knows
the difference. He knows the Colonel doesn't, doesn't
care, in fact—the Bloodless Third has come
for blood, for a victory in a year when nothing else
will do. They can't think any farther than their balls.
They're a brace of bulldogs straining at the leash

but it's the dogs below that give the first alarm—
a yip, a bark, a howl or two, then
duets, trios, soprano howls, tenor
yawps, a rising canon of mutts and mongrels
no one could sleep through. Except they do sleep through,
deep in a dream of trust because their Chief
Black Kettle smoked a peace pipe two months since
with Soule and the other officers, then saved the lives
of a hundred twenty troopers on the Smoky
Hill, and sleeps now with the Stars and Stripes
as keepsake by his pipe. The one who trusts the most
now sound asleep in the arms of his belief

as Soule counts off the seconds. Minutes. An Indian
woman steps from a lodge and gives a long
appraising look, then turns her head downstream
to where the Cheyennes keep their ponies tethered,
then back at them again. What does she think?
That they're a herd of buffalo, come from the Smoky Hill?
His heart is strangely moved by her delay.
It is as if the truth of what they are
must fight its way brain cell by brain cell while she gazes,
the promises, the treaties, peace pipes, blankets, gifts
thrust aside by a gleam of steel in morning
sunlight. She puts her head back, raises up her arms . . .

He is asleep. He is talking to Coyote. Coyote is inside
Buffalo's skull. He has made himself small
to be the master of small spaces, to dance and sing
about himself, about his trickster ways.
He says "Come out, Coyote, come out I tell you."
Coyote keeps on dancing. "You're dancing on a pitfall."
Coyote laughs, "Oh no I'm not. Never
do I dance in a manscent. But you, Black Kettle,
where do you dance? This land in the hook of the curve
of Sandy Creek—isn't it a skull drawn
in sand? But where are its bones? The capsules of its eyes?
Whose scent do you dance and sing in, under the moon?"

He hears what Coyote says. He hears it heavily.
But he doesn't leave his sleep. Not yet. There is more
to ask of Coyote. He feels it. But what? He feels
it somewhere, but not upon his tongue. Somewhere
between his ears and eyes and mouth but not
upon his tongue. His enemy, slowness of speech.

That is why he waits to hear what Coyote says,
the master trickster always twenty paces
out ahead. Not the bravest, not
the best, but out before. As a young man, how
he wished to ride in front. And now like cottonwood
his wishes fill the winds with drifting feathers.

Coyote keeps on talking but his voice
is high and thin and fading. He can see that Coyote's
jaws are moving. That smile of his, that little
shake of his head in confidence. It makes him lean
down closer. There are tiny drummers, he can hear
them now, Coyote's kinsmen gathering in
from the flyways of geese and crane, from the runs
of prairie dog and rabbit. How can they squeeze
in such a space? And yet they seem to keep on
coming. A hubbub. He can hear the click
of bones as they bet their luck, he wants to cry out
and joke and boast with the best of Coyote's kin

but *eeeyaah* is what he hears, the little lighted
skull, the drummers, singers, dancers, gone.
A smell of ashes, buffalo robes, and dark.
Eeeyaah it comes again, he knows the voice
of Crow Woman, the rising note that stops in the back
of her throat, the warning note that brings him up
and running to the opening where he sees
her standing still as a blasted tree, her arms
extended at the ring of sand hills above the Creek.
There is a glint of light on steel, feathers
of breath from men and horses spinning upward,
a whinny, then a mule's complaint, then a shout

and the line of horsemen starts to spill over
the slope. He sounds Crow Woman's cry, then
again, and the camp has come alive with moving
men and women. He springs inside
his lodge, seizes his lance, the flag, and a white
linen rag. He ties the two of them to the shaft
and sweeps it back outside, raising it high
to the peak of his lodgepole where the wind unfurls them both.
The flag. Their very flag. And the flag of peace.
Together. He can see the columns riding toward them.
Mounted. Some are Blue Coats, their sabres drawn.
The high-pitched yells, the bugles. And now, the shooting.

Bruce Cutler is the author of *The Year of the Green Wave, Two Long Poems, The Doctrine of Selective Depravity,* and three plays. Cutler's work has appeared in *Poetry, Poetry Northwest, Yale Review, Shenandoah,* and *New Letters*; he has been awarded a Bush Art Fellowship, an NEA Creative Writing Fellowship in Poetry, and a grant from the Witter Bynner Foundation for Poetry. He lives in St. Paul, Minnesota.

An excerpt from

Go by Go

a mystery by Jon A. Jackson

GROUNDHOG DAY IN 1951, in Butte, was brilliantly sunny. Any fat little rodent would need sunglasses if he ventured out of his burrow, but he'd also need an extra fur hat and coat, in the view of Special Agent Senkpiel. It was brutally cold, minus-27 degrees F. at one p.m. Senkpiel tugged on galoshes, wrapped a wool muffler about his neck, turned up the collar of his heavy tweed overcoat, pulled on rabbit fur-lined gloves and arranged earmuffs under his felt fedora before he dared step outside the regional office of the Federal Bureau of Investigation. By the time he reached his government Ford, his bones were cold. This was the eighth straight day that the mercury had not gotten above minus ten, and Senkpiel wasn't used to it. It got cold in Grand Rapids, Michigan, where he was from, but it never got so damn cold and it never stayed this cold for so damn long. People around Butte always said it was a dry cold, not that nasty damp cold of the Midwest. But when it got this cold and stayed that way, what the hell difference could it make? He had begun to feel an edge of panic: maybe it would never get warm again.

Somehow he coaxed the frozen car to a reluctant stuttering life and heel-and-toed the brake and accelerator down Montana Avenue to the "flat," as Butteants called the residential area that lay below the Hill on which the old part of the city was built. It was even colder down here, he thought, the cold presses down. He found the street he wanted and parked in front of a small, white clapboard house. He turned off the ignition reluctantly, fearful that the engine would never revive.

The woman who answered the door was wearing a heavy sweater that didn't begin to obscure an enormous bosom. Steamy clouds billowed out the door bearing a cloying odor of fuel oil. She was a stout woman of about sixty, with red hair that was trying to turn gray but not succeeding, thanks to copious applications of henna rinse. To say that Agent Senkpiel found her unattractive was inaccurate: he thought her repulsive. She might have been a beauty, a long time ago, but Senkpiel was too young to see it. To him she was old and fat and ugly. She wore too much makeup and wasn't at all tidy. She shouldn't be allowed to wear slacks, the agent thought. Not unless she lost thirty or forty pounds.

The woman brought in tea and then seated herself in an upholstered platform rocker next to the heater. The windows were frosted to mere luminosity. She rummaged in the enormous bosom of her sweater and drew out a pack of Lucky Strikes. She offered them to the agent. He declined. She lit up and began to puff the first of ten or so that she would smoke during the interview.

She poured tea for both of them, and then, to the agent's amazement, produced a pint of brandy and offered to "sweeten" his tea.

"No thank you," he declared emphatically.

She shrugged and poured a generous amount into her own teacup.

Agent Senkpiel explained that he had been asked by a Federal Agency, which he would not specify, to make certain inquiries. Mrs. Ritter was under no obligation to answer the questions, but he, Agent Senkpiel, was obliged to record all of her answers for report, including refusals to answer. Mrs. Ritter nodded and asked what it was all about. Agent Senkpiel said he didn't know, which was approximately true; he was simply required to ask several questions. Could they begin?

Mrs. Ritter took a hearty sip of her "tea," smacked her lips, and said, "fire away, laddie." She had a faint, very faint Irish tang to her speech. It wasn't uncommon in Butte, as he'd noticed long since.

She caused him consternation right away, by denying that she was the estranged wife of Goodwin Ritter.

"We never really got married," she explained cheerfully. "I was married to Mr. Paton, you see. But I ran off with Goody and we had a kid and I didn't want the kid to be a bastard, so we just said we were married. Nobody ever questioned it."

"He listed you as his wife on his military records," the agent said. "You were paid his Army allotment."

"So sue me," Mrs. Ritter said.

"It could be more serious than that. I don't know the statutes right offhand, but I'm sure it's a federal offense."

She thrust out her thin wrists, jangling with hoops of gold and brass, as if eager to be manacled. Then she laughed and puffed her cigarette. She went on like this, throughout the interview, clowning and carrying on.

Agent Senkpiel was irritated, at first. He never perceived her anxiety, especially whenever he touched on the events surrounding Goodwin Ritter's initial visit to Butte, or when he mentioned "known Communists," such as Frank Little.

Mrs. Ritter staunchly maintained that she had never known Frank Little, although she'd heard about him, of course. She had never heard Goody mention Mr. Little, she averred, and as far as she knew Goody had never met the man.

"Goody was a detective, like you," she said. "He worked for the Pinks. The Pinkertons. I don't know what he did—strike-breaking, I guess—but I'm sure he never came into contact with Frank Little."

The agent bored in on the subject, but got little more out of her. And gradually, at first to her relief, but finally to her surprise, she realized that the FBI was not particularly interested in Frank Little. They were only interested in Goody, in some kind of roundabout way.

So what was the FBI on about, she wondered? She decided that this must be something to do with the Army. Goody must be doing something for the Army, a movie perhaps. This was a whatchamacallit, a security check, she thought. Security checks were a fact of life, anymore.

At this point, she began to relax and have fun. She had a lot more brandy and lapsed into misty nostalgia about Goody Ritter. "Oh, he was a lovely boy," she said, more than once, shaking her head. "He was good for all night, that one."

As for Communism, she couldn't remember him ever mentioning it. "He was more a bosom man, if you ask me," she said, with a wink—she pronounced it "boozum", with her characteristic Irish tang.

Richard Senkpiel was amused, despite his professional misgivings, his apprehensions about the astounding cold, his general unhappiness. He didn't enjoy being an FBI agent in Butte. He was twenty-eight years old and had expected to be in Washington, D.C., by now. He'd been in the Bureau for two years. Things seemed a little tight, promotion-wise, but the post-war Communist conspiracy augured well. He had decided that if he wasn't moved up the ladder by the end of the fiscal year, he would go back to law school. Another side to his character was a certain Midwestern romanticism. It was why, in fact, he'd joined the FBI. He'd actually believed the "gang-busters" stuff he'd read in pulp magazines and heard on the radio. He believed in J. Edgar Hoover's public campaigns against Communism. But, he'd soon discovered that the FBI was nothing like that. Of course, one doesn't really expect it to be, but there was no gang-busting, no running down of spies, none. It was boring.

Thus, he was entertained to discover that Sheila Ritter (Sheila Paton, that is) actually was acquainted with the actors Edward G. Robinson and George Raft.

"Eddie is a wonderful guy, a real gentleman," she told Senkpiel. "He's an art collector, you know. Mmmhmm. You wouldn't think so. Jewish. And the sweetest manners; not a tough guy, at all. He's not what you'd call handsome, but oh! those bedroom eyes! That 'Rico' stuff is all malarkey. Tiny little feet he has, and perfect toes. I didn't like Georgie at first. He tried to get in my slacks within a half-hour! But we soon got that straightened out and he's still a good friend. He was a hoofer, you know. A dancer. I think it was Jack Warner, or one of those cretins, who thought he'd make a good gangster. Of course, we didn't know any of these chaps when we first went to Hollywood, but Goody soon was chumming around with Coop and Clark and . . ."

"You don't mean Gary Cooper and Clark Gable?" Senkpiel interrupted.

"Who else? Coop's from Montana, you know. Over around Helena, or someplace. Myrna's from over there, too. God, I hated her! What a snoot, and she's nothing but a high school girl who ran away from Montana. Anyway, Coop used to come over and we'd gab about Butte. He's crazy about hunting and fishing and he's forever gabbing about getting back up here. I dare say he does, once in awhile, but I never see him. Goody played poker with him and Clark and Papa till all hours. I'll tell you one thing, that Hemingway is an awful shit. He was a horrible influence on all of them. They all drank too much anyway."

Senkpiel was rapt. The next time she offered the brandy he accepted some in his tea. It didn't taste so awful. Besides, it was so damned cold out and so warm and cozy inside.

She told him how they had spent the early years of their so-called married life in San Francisco, after Goody had gotten out of the Army. "He got gassed, you know. It affected his lungs."

Senkpiel wondered how Ritter had gotten gassed, since he'd never left the States and never been in a war zone. Indeed, Goodwin Ritter had only been in the Army for a few months. But the Agent let it pass. It wasn't his business to inform informants.

"I worked as a waitress to support him, while he wrote," Sheila told him. "It was quite a strain, with all the kids. Goody wasn't awfully good with them, I'm afraid." She sighed and took a gulp of spiked tea. "I'd come home from the restaurant and find Elaine and Devvy running up and down Post street at ten at night! And the little one, Alex, crying in his crib with shit all over his little ass! And Goody typing away and smoking, which he shouldn't have done—because of his lungs, you see—and blind to it all! None of them would have eaten a scrap all day."

"Did he have any Communist friends in San Francisco?"

"Communists? No. He went about with cops and bums and crooks, and sometimes he did a little job of work for the Pinks—the Pinkertons, not the Commies." She shook her head, ruefully. "Still, it was the best time. People always say that, I know, and it sounds so silly, but it was the best time. Later on, when he got famous and we had lots of money, it wasn't the same. He was having it off with all these young girls—starlets, you know—and was never home much. By then we'd had Molly. I finally got fed up and came back here."

Senkpiel ignored her language, although it would have shocked him, a teapot earlier. "Why'd you come back here?" he asked. "You're not a native of Montana." Butte was not a place to come back to, in his mind. He was constantly astonished by the ferocity of the locals' devotion to the place.

"Migod, I wasn't going back to Ireland, was I?" she said. "I have a boy who lives here. He's a poet, you know. He writes lovely poetry about the mines. He won't leave Butte."

"It was your first husband who was a Communist, then?" Senkpiel asked, struggling back to his task.

"Why do you go on so about the Communists? Nobody is a Communist in this country. Why would they be? Now, Sean, he belonged to the I. W. W. Is that Communist? I thought it was before Communism. It was supposed to be a labor union. Poor Seanie, he thought the sun rose and set in Frank Little's ass—" she covered her mouth with her hand, in mock embarassment, adding "—not that my Sean was queer, or anything like that. Why he was as straight as a poker. And as hard." She laughed, girlishly.

Senkpiel smiled, but doggedly pursued what appeared to be a promising vein of information. "Were Ritter and your husband associates? I mean, were they good friends?"

"They were bosom buddies. Well, they fell out over me, of course, especially when I ran off to California with Goody. But they made it up. Sean came out to stay with us, after a bit, from time to time. I believe he still sees Goody. It was Goody who got Sean into the movie business."

Senkpiel perked up. "I didn't know Mr. Paton was in the movies," he said.

"Sean's a rigger, or was. He's pretty much retired now. But he still takes on a job now and then, if the pay is good. Oh, he was famous! Probably the best rigger in Hollywood."

Senkpiel had no idea what a rigger was and rather than expose his ignorance he passed that over for a few questions about the curious relationship between Mrs. Ritter (or Paton, as it were) and the two men. "Wasn't Mr. Paton jealous?" This was irrelevant to his inquiry, of course, but he was intrigued.

"At first," Sheila admitted. "But he saw how it was. I was just crazy for Goody. And then, well we had a kind of private arrangement ourselves." She smiled slyly.

"Did Ritter know about this, uh, private arrangement between you and your, uh, husband?"

"Not likely! Goody would've blown his top. He was very jealous . . . though it was all right for him to go out and screw every slut in Hollywood, and I wasn't to say a word! Well, two can play at that game. I made it a point to have it off with every single friend of his—Coop, Georgie, Bogie, all of them. Well, not Eddie. Eddie was too much of a gentleman."

Senkpiel was flabbergasted. "You mean you, uh, went with Gary Cooper? And the others?" When Sheila smiled knowingly, he pushed on. "With Clark Gable? You did?" He believed her. In fact, it was obvious that she wasn't lying. She must have been something to see, he thought, and not so very long ago, after all. "Did Mr. Ritter realize this was going on?"

"I didn't exactly advertise it in Billboard," Sheila said, with a lascivious grin, "but I know it got back to him. There are no secrets in Hollywood, that's for sure. Your reputation's more secure up on Mercury, in Venus Alley," she gestured toward the Hill. "And that is surely why I'm sitting here in this wretched hovel in

Butte, instead of the beach house in Santa Monica. Not that I mind Butte—I've always loved Butte . . . Butte people are real people. But I could be better situated—up on the Hill, perhaps, on Silver Street, or out by the Country Club."

Agent Senkpiel unconsciously rubbed his ears. Was she making this up? He had conducted several interviews and interrogations, but he'd never heard anything like this. He concluded she was telling the truth. The lives of people like Ritter, and Sheila, were simply different from those of ordinary folks. She probably didn't think it was extraordinary. He wanted to ask her about Bogart, but he couldn't. It wasn't in him.

"This friendship between Mr. Paton and Mr. Ritter," Senkpiel said, "did your husband influence Ritter toward Communism? Did they talk about socialism and that sort of thing?"

"Sean? Influence Goody?" Sheila laughed. She poured herself more tea and brandy and offered a refill to Senkpiel. He accepted it—"just a little." She slopped his cup full.

"Sean could never influence Goody," she said. "They're just pals, the way so many men are in America." She eyed Senkpiel shrewdly. "They're like boys, aren't they? Though, I must admit, Goody is more of a man than any of them. Or was. He's not in good health, they say."

"I would think you'd resent Ritter, now. After having supported him during his struggle, to be . . ." Senkpiel gestured at the surroundings.

"Not so much as some might," she said. "He wrote the stories, after all. I couldn't have written them. You couldn't. I don't even think Goody can write them, anymore. But I shouldn't say that. He's surprised me all along. I never thought we'd go so far and do so much. I knew it was going to be better than staying with Sean, but I'd have gone anyway. And I had a good time. Goody supported us well when the money came, and he still sends money. He's been real good about Molly. She's an airline stewardess, you know. And now, I have Seanie. He's a comfort."

"But Ritter has treated you so shabbily, it seems," Senkpiel protested.

"He's a lovely man," she insisted. "Goody isn't exactly a Milord Percy, but he's got guts, when it comes down to it. He is generous, by his own standards. He never asked for a lot, but he took whatever was given and enjoyed it. It's not a bad philosophy, such as it is. If I asked for more, I'm sure he'd give me more, whatever I asked. But I don't ask."

Senkpiel poked around a bit more, inquiring about possible Communist influences and associations of Goodwin Ritter, but finally he gave it up and they whiled away the afternoon with Sheila's ribald reminiscences of Cooper and others. About four o'clock, Sean Paton, junior, the poet, came home from the bars. He was a huge fellow in his late thirties, a little thick in the hips and red of lip, and more than a bit tipsy, but pleased to find his mother and a friend in like condition. The three of them sat down to a little serious drinking and Senkpiel had to be driven home, ostensibly because his car wouldn't start.

The next morning it was warmer. The cold spell had been broken. But Senkpiel's head felt broken, as well. Like a good FBI agent, however, he struggled down to the office and began to draft his report.

"The subject," he noted, "seems to have an active fantasy life and is possibly an alcoholic, however a few comments emerged that may be of significance in this investigation . . ."

JON A. JACKSON is the author of three previous mysteries: *The Diehard, The Blind Pig,* and *Grootka.* A new work, *Hit on the House,* will be published by Atlantic Monthly Press in January of 1993 and Atlantic Monthly plans to reprint his first two works in the near future. He lives in Corvallis, Montana.

Acknowledgments

I WOULD LIKE TO THANK Lea Chatham for allowing this book to be made (and allowing me to walk at Deep Creek) and Sally Epps for trying to add her spotty memory to my shoddy one. Belated but eternal thanks to the people I was lucky enough to work with—Stacy Sandler, Janice Kimmel, Cindy Murphy, Dick Murphy, Laurel Desnick, and (too late) Kevin Morrissey—as well as all the people at other independent presses and bookstores who tried to steer us right and cushion our fall. Anne Garner, a graphic designer and a professor at Montana State University, and Christine Taylor, of Wilsted & Taylor in Oakland, made these books both beautiful and possible. Thanks to Glenn Godward, the world's best bartender, for the Livingston Bar & Grille menus, and to Stephen Potenberg for his patience during those years. And most deeply, and often too late, a thank-you to all the writers we published, and those who were ready to take a chance on the future.

Then, after the accident there and at the end of that summer, he answered again the obscure call and vanished into the wilderness of the south. "I wish I knew where I was going," he wrote Jeanne Carr at the outset of that long walk. "'Doomed to be carried of the spirit into the wilderness,' I suppose. I wish I could be more moderate in my desires, but I cannot, and so there is no

Moving ever higher towards some transfiguration, he climbed into and then out of the shadow of death, as on his ascent of Mt. Ritter, which he knew he shouldn't attempt but felt driven to try. On this occasion he found himself, as he later wrote, "brought to a dead stop, with arms outspread, clinging close to the face of the rock, unable to move hand or foot either up or down. My doom appeared fixed. I *must* fall." But he did not, later attributing his rescue to the visitation of some inspiriting power that directed his actions. Up in these mountains the world's weary roar was only a rumor he heard occasionally from visitors—travelers' tales of strife in the dusty places far below. And he found confirmation

I think the